Claire wanted to call Dean, to hear his voice

But she had to figure out why she felt this way.

For twenty-five years she'd dreamed of going to college. That was a long time. Why hadn't she?

She'd told herself her family came first. But was it something else?

Maybe subconsciously she felt she'd made a mistake by getting pregnant the first time and was trying to atone by sacrificing her own goals. Did she feel she didn't deserve to have her dream come true?

Her thoughts angered her and she had no answers. All she knew was that first she had to accept the pregnancy. After that, she wasn't sure about her life. Maybe the dream was just that—a dream.

And it was time to let it go.

Dear Reader,

I'm always asked where I get my story ideas—this book was actually a very nice gift. I was sitting in a beauty shop listening to the conversations going on around me. A stylist was telling her client about a friend in her forties who had just found out she was pregnant. Her youngest child had just graduated from college.

I found this intriguing and, yes, I kept listening. Seems the friend had gotten pregnant and married young, and instead of going to college she devoted her life to her family. Now that her kids were grown, she'd enrolled for the fall semester. But history repeated itself and she was again faced with an unplanned pregnancy. She had packed a suitcase and left. Everyone, especially her husband, was worried.

This bit of beauty-shop gossip grabbed me, and I really felt for this unknown woman. I thought it would make a great story.

When writing this, I had a lot of blanks to fill in. I asked friends how they'd feel if they had gotten pregnant in their forties, and I didn't get one positive response. Everyone loved their kids but didn't relish the idea of having a child late in life. I never found out what happened to the stylist's friend, but I hope she made all the right choices, like Claire and Dean. As I dealt with their lives, it touched a lot of emotional chords in me. I hope you enjoy this gift.

Warmly,

Linda Warren

P.S. It always brightens my day to hear from readers. You can e-mail me at Lw1508@aol.com or write me at P.O. Box 5182, Bryan, TX 77805 or visit my Web site at www.lindawarren.net or www.myspace.com/authorlindawarren. Your letters will be answered.

ALWAYS A MOTHER
Linda Warren

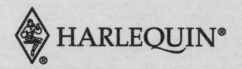

TORONTO • NEW YORK • LONDON
AMSTERDAM • PARIS • SYDNEY • HAMBURG
STOCKHOLM • ATHENS • TOKYO • MILAN • MADRID
PRAGUE • WARSAW • BUDAPEST • AUCKLAND

ISBN-13: 978-0-373-71499-5
ISBN-10: 0-373-71499-8

ALWAYS A MOTHER

This edition published by arrangement with Harlequin Books S.A.

® and TM are trademarks of the publisher. Trademarks indicated with ® are registered in the United States Patent and Trademark Office, the Canadian Trade Marks Office and in other countries.

www.eHarlequin.com

Printed in U.S.A.

ABOUT THE AUTHOR

Award-winning, bestselling author Linda Warren has written twenty-one books for Harlequin Superromance and Harlequin American Romance. She grew up in the farming and ranching community of Smetana, Texas, the only girl in a family of boys. She loves to write about Texas, and from time to time scenes and characters from her childhood show up in her books. Linda lives in College Station, Texas, not far from her birthplace, with her husband, Billy, and a menagerie of wild animals, from Canada geese to bobcats. Visit her Web site at www.lindawarren.net.

Books by Linda Warren

I dedicate this book to mothers everywhere.
And to my mother, Mary Dudake Siegert.
Thanks for the freedom to dream, a spirit to believe
and roots to keep me grounded.

ACKNOWLEDGMENTS

A special thanks to Robin Fuller, Amy Landry,
Dorothy Kissman and Phyllis Fletcher for their help
in the writing of this book.

Thanks, too, to the American Heart Association and
U.S. Department of Health and Human Services.

Any errors are strictly mine
and all characters are fictional.

CHAPTER ONE

CLAIRE RENNELS CLUNG to one thought.

She couldn't be sick.

Not now.

But the waves of chills shuddering across her clammy skin told their own story. She shivered and crumpled to the bathroom floor like cheap toilet paper. Clutching the commode, she felt beads of perspiration break out on her forehead, and took several quick breaths.

What was wrong with her?

She drew another long breath, slowly releasing it through her mouth. Feeling calmer, she tipped her head back against the flowery wallpaper and stared up at the peach-colored ceiling. They needed to paint. The color had faded to a shade she couldn't describe, and a spiderweb dangled in one corner.

Someone, preferably not her, should clean away the cobwebs. She wasn't a great housekeeper and would be the first to admit that failing. Their home had a lived-in look, but it was comfortable and cheery.

The calm didn't last long. Bile rose in her throat and her stomach spun with gut-wrenching nausea. She leaned over the toilet, retching one more time. She should be with her husband, Dean, helping to move his mom into a new house, but here she was, puking her guts out and getting acquainted with the ceiling.

With her stomach finally resting, she pushed herself to her feet, stumbled to the sink and washed out her sour mouth. She should clean the bathroom, but she didn't have the strength at the moment. Maybe later.

Glancing at herself in the mirror, she did a double take. Holy cow! Her pallid skin, fatigued eyes and sweat-soaked hair made her look like death warmed over, as Bunny, her mother-in-law, would say.

Back to bed, no question. Claire planned to hide her weak body beneath the covers until the world was a brighter shade of hearty pink, not sickly green.

As she trudged toward the bedroom she kept repeating her delusional mantra for the day: *I'm not sick. I'm not.*

Suddenly a thought occurred to her and she stopped dead in her tracks. When was the last time she'd had her period? She quickly calculated the weeks.

Her hand trembled as she scrubbed at her face. *Think. Think. Think.* She'd had a period in late June, right before they'd taken their daughters, Sarah and Samantha, to Cancun for a family vacation. Since Sarah was getting into a serious relationship, this would probably be the last trip with just the four of them.

Claire made her way to the bed and sank down on it, dragging her fingers through her sweaty hair. This was late August. *No. No. No.* She couldn't be pregnant, not at the age of forty-three. Life couldn't be that cruel. But she knew that it could.

Staggering to her feet, she dug in a drawer for jogging pants and a T-shirt. She had to buy a pregnancy test even if she threw up all the way to the store.

TWENTY MINUTES LATER she rushed into her bathroom to perform the test, sincerely hoping this was one she'd fail.

Staring at the result, Claire moaned and slid to the floor, tears streaming down her cheeks. *Not again!* How could she be so careless?

Swiping away tears, she rested against the vanity. In a little over a week she would start college, her dream since she was eighteen. She'd managed to earn a few credits while she'd raised her family, and now she would finally get her degree. But just like when she was eighteen, she found herself pregnant.

Her stomach cramped again, this time from the selfish, negative emotions swamping her. She'd raised two wonderful daughters and put them and her husband through college. She'd earned the right to do something for herself for a change.

She stared into the bedroom to a bookshelf adorned with baby pictures of their daughters. Set among them were trophies and awards she and Dean had won in high school. He'd been a football jock and she'd been salutatorian of the class. The hunk and the nerd, they were called. But as smart as she was supposed to be, she wasn't smart enough to avoid getting pregnant.

At age eighteen, two months from graduation, Claire had discovered she was going to have a baby. All her hopes and dreams crumbled as she made the hardest decision of her life. She wasn't going through that again.

This time she was older, although not much wiser. She knew she had options. She should call Dean, but if she saw him she might actually kill him. It was her body and she'd make this decision alone.

You didn't create the baby alone, a little voice whispered inside her head. She wouldn't listen to that voice. It had told her to go ahead and use a condom when she'd forgotten her diaphragm on the Cancun trip. She might kill the little voice, too.

After gathering the packaging and the pregnancy test paraphernalia, Claire hurried to the kitchen, wrapped everything in paper towels, and threw it into the trash to hide the evidence. She wasn't ready to tell Dean. She ran to her car before she could change her mind.

The Planned Parenthood Clinic wasn't far away. She'd driven by it many times, and sometimes thought of the women inside. She'd never understood how a woman could abort a baby. This was different, though. This was *her* life. Beyond that, she wouldn't let herself think.

She parked some distance away, and took a few moments to calm down. Protesters marched outside in the August heat. A wrought-iron security fence enclosed the clinic to keep the protesters out and to protect the women who made the choice to abort their child.

All Claire had to do was go inside, take another pregnancy test and make a decision. Easy.

Wrong. She'd been raised in a Christian home, just as she and Dean had raised their girls. She took a deep breath and prayed for strength. The moment she did, she knew this was wrong—so horribly wrong. She couldn't do it. Her beliefs wouldn't allow it.

She had rights. Was that supposed to alleviate the guilt? She tucked her blond hair behind her ear. In reality, her rights had been compromised the moment she'd agreed to have sex with her husband.

She knew, as did Dean, that a condom wasn't one hundred percent safe. There was always a risk of conception, and once she and Dean had taken that risk they had to be prepared to deal with the consequences.

Just as they had years ago.

Claire rested her hand on her stomach. The new life inside took precedence over her rights. Some people might not believe that, but she did. No way could she end her pregnancy. She couldn't do it when she was eighteen, and she certainly couldn't do it now.

Slowly, she drove home, trying to come to terms with everything she was feeling. Talking to Dean wasn't going to help. She knew him as well as she knew herself. He'd offer his support, but what she needed now was time alone. He wasn't going to understand that. Still, she hurriedly threw clothes into a carryall.

Grabbing underwear out of a drawer, she saw a stack of old letters tied with a worn red ribbon hidden away in the back. She pulled them out. These were letters she'd written to Dean in high school and after they were married. He'd kept them in a drawer in his bedroom. When she'd moved in with him and his mother, she'd found them, and was so touched he'd saved them. She'd tied the red ribbon around the letters adding new ones to the pile over the years. Writing to Dean always gave her peace and strength, and reinforced their love.

Love letters.

Her love letters.

Her feelings. Her emotions.

Twice in the past she'd faced unexpected pregnancies and had found acceptance waiting deep in her heart. She had to find that once again.

Everything she'd felt for Dean was in the letters, her

fears, her hopes, her dreams, but most of all her love. Looking at them, she knew that to come to terms with her future she would have to find the love and motivation that had defined her life. The letters would do that. She gently placed them in the bag.

In the kitchen, she wrote a note for Dean.

Dean,
I'm not feeling well and need to get out of the city for a while. Don't worry. I'll call.
Claire

At the moment that was the best she could do. She'd phone him later and try to explain. Right now she didn't need to hear him say they could work this out or that he loved her. She just needed some time to herself. She paused as she saw her new laptop lying on the desk—the laptop Dean had bought her to start college. Swallowing back a sob, she ran for the door.

She had no idea where she was going until she got on the North MoPac Expressway and saw US 290. Claire and Dean had bought a small house on Lake Travis, just northwest of Austin, when Sarah was about twelve. They had a friend who'd been getting a divorce, and all they had to do was come up with five thousand dollars cash and take up the payments for the next ten years. It was a very good deal and Claire had known that if they took it, their budget would not extend for her return to college. But that was okay. Her family came first. They'd spent a lot of time on the lake ever since, especially with the girls and their friends. Their summers were always fun.

Without a second thought she took the exit and headed

for the lake house now, hoping to recapture a part of her youth and maybe a part of herself.

DEAN RENNELS STROLLED through the back door, whistling. He'd finally gotten his mom moved. She'd been living in the same house he'd grown up in. As a single mother, she'd worked extra hard to make sure he was raised in a good environment. Back then the neighborhood was nice and the park a place to play ball.

In the last few years, though, the area had gone downhill, the park was used for drug deals and the neighborhood kids were no longer safe. Neither was his mom, who'd refused to move until a teenage girl was murdered in the park.

Her new town house had just been built, and updated with a security system—everything he wanted for his mother, the only person who'd been there for him and Claire in the early days.

He threw his keys on the desk in the kitchen, hoping Claire was feeling better. He was sure it was only nerves. There were only ten days until she started college, a dream she'd had since she was eighteen. The reality was hard for her to believe, but he was going to make sure nothing stood in the way of her dream this time.

Nothing.

"Honey," he called, walking toward the bedroom. He picked up the comforter from the hardwood floor and laid it on the rumpled bed. In the bathroom, a stench sent him reeling. She was definitely sick. Where was she? A sliver of alarm slid up his spine. Could she have driven herself to the hospital? No. She would have called him.

Hurrying back to the kitchen, he spotted the note attached to the refrigerator. He read it, frowning. "What…?"

He read it again, but it still didn't tell him a lot. She needed to get away. Why? His gut tightened with a premonition. Something was wrong.

He dragged in a breath. Claire had said she'd call, so he had to wait. To keep busy, he went into the utility room for cleaning supplies to scrub the bathroom. That done, he sprayed air freshener, something the girls had bought at a specialty shop. He sniffed. Lime and verbena. Not bad. But not something he wanted to smell on a regular basis.

After straightening the bed, he flipped on the TV. An Austin high school team was supposed to be playing on one of the cable channels. He found it. Pivoting, he started for the den and noticed Claire's underwear drawer. She'd left it open, and the contents were spilling out. A spot was vacant in the back corner—where Claire stored the love letters. He teased her about keeping them, but she'd said one day their daughters might like to read about their parents' lives as teenagers.

Why had Claire taken the letters? They'd been there for years. He closed the drawer with a sinking feeling. Had she left him? No. There were no signs. They were in love, always had been since grade school.

He'd sat behind her in class and had a bird's-eye view of her blond ponytail and the colorful ribbons tied around it. Every day brought a different ribbon, to match her clothes. As a boy, he didn't quite get that.

But he got Claire, even though she tended to ignore him. So one day he yanked her ribbon and drew her full attention. She'd quickly retied the bow and glared at him. He just grinned at her.

Later he'd yanked it again on the playground and run away. She'd yelled after him, "I'll get you, Dean Rennels."

And she did. Over the next few years she got him in more ways than he could remember. Claire was a voracious reader and won the reading award every term, writing the most book reports of anyone in their class. In ninth grade the teacher wanted them to read with a buddy, and the top readers had the honor of choosing their partners. Claire picked him, the boy'd who pulled her ribbons. The guys teased him, but he didn't care. Usually he couldn't wait to get out of class to go play ball, but for the first time, something, or someone, held him back.

After that Claire helped him with his book reports and made suggestions of what he might want to read. She introduced him to Tom Sawyer and Huckleberry Finn. He'd loved those stories, but couldn't quite get into *The Grapes of Wrath* or *Moby Dick* or *Wuthering Heights* and many other books she couldn't put down.

It wasn't just the books; it was Claire with her soft lilting voice, her serene expression and the light in her brown eyes. He never noticed those things in other girls, but Claire held him spellbound, which was a feat because sports usually had his undivided attention.

The School Dance, 1980

DEAN'S LOCKER WAS ACROSS from Claire's. The school dance was a week away and he wasn't sure about going. Since he played football, the coach said he had to go. Dean wasn't sure why. The dance had nothing to do with football.

As Claire arranged books neatly in her locker, he walked over to her. "Are you going to the dance?"

"No. My parents don't allow me to date."

"My mom won't let me date, either, but I'm thinking about going."

She closed her locker, but before she could walk away, he blurted out, "Maybe we could meet at the dance. It wouldn't exactly be a date."

A smile turned up the corners of her mouth and he knew he was in love, or something. He felt happy and ill at the same time.

"Okay." Her smile broadened. "I'll meet you at the dance."

He was nervous getting ready that evening. He was very careful not to go outside or even pick up a ball. No way was he getting mud on his clothes tonight.

His mom, Margaret Ann Rennels, better known as Bunny, drove him to the dance. She stopped her Ford Fairmont at the school. "Behave yourself," she said, crushing out a cigarette in the ashtray.

"Do you have to smoke? I don't want to smell like that. It's gross."

"I have the window down and I don't smoke in the house. Isn't that enough?"

"I guess." Dean twisted the rearview mirror so he could peer at himself. "Do I look okay?"

Bunny frowned at him. "What's wrong with you? You never care how you look."

"This is a dance. I'm supposed to look nice."

She touched his cheek. "You're handsome just like that no-good father of yours."

He groaned, not wanting to talk about his dad, who'd left them before Dean was born. The man couldn't handle the responsibility of a baby. Bunny said he was shot a few years later by a jealous husband, but every time she thought about him she drank heavily. Dean hoped she wasn't doing that tonight. Although tonight she had to go to work at her job as a waitress, so she wouldn't be drinking.

"I'll be back at ten. If I'm late, stay put. I'll be here."

"Yes, ma'am."

"And, champ, don't worry. The girls will fall over themselves to dance with you."

He wasn't worried about other girls, only Claire. Her parents were wealthy, her father a lawyer, and Dean knew there was no way they'd be allowed to date. But tonight he was going to dance with her.

The moment he saw her, his stomach lurched, as it did every time he managed to catch a pass he thought was out of his reach. In a pink dress, with her blond hair hanging down her back, she reminded him of Cinderella, a ridiculous fairy tale Bunny used to read to him. Dean wanted to be Claire's prince and that frightened him, because he'd never had thoughts like that before. He considered running out of the gym, but she walked over to him and all he could do was stare.

The music started and he took her hand. They did all the crazy moves, laughing and joking, and then a slow number came on. As he held her he knew he was in love. He was just a kid, but he still knew.

DEAN PACED.
Claire, where are you?

CLAIRE SHOVED HER KEY into the lock and opened the door at the lake house. The heat was stifling and she quickly turned on the air-conditioning. As cool air wafted from the vents, she carried her bag to a bedroom, though she didn't know how long she was staying.

Long enough to accept her future.

She put the perishable foods she'd picked up at a convenience store in the refrigerator, and left the other groceries on the counter. Tugging on a pair of shorts and a tank top, she realized her body was already going through changes. A month ago the shorts fit fine. Now... She grabbed suntan lotion and hurried out to the pier. Their lot sloped down to the water's edge. She sat cross-legged on the planks and methodically, without thinking, applied lotion to her arms, legs and face. Her fingers smoothed over a tiny lump of cellulite and she stopped. Damn! She was too old to have a baby.

What was she going to do? She wasn't a frightened eighteen-year-old. As a mature woman who had learned to be strong, independent and resourceful, she should find this easy.

But it wasn't.

Sunlight danced off the rippling water with a blinding array of sparks, warming and refreshing at the same time. She breathed in the clean air. Since it was Friday, the lake was busy with boats, skiers and swimmers, but their house was secluded in a cove among gnarled oak trees, away from the crowd. People were making the most of the last weekend before school started. Public schools, that is. College started the following Monday.

The afternoon sun heated her skin and her thoughts.

She was pregnant for the third time, at age forty-three.

All sorts of emotions engulfed her—denial, anger, confusion, defiance, anxiety and fear. How could she accept this? How could she not? She ran her hands up her arms as a feeling of déjà vu came over her.

At eighteen, she'd been frightened and worried. Being

older didn't change those feelings, except she was angry
with herself because she knew better than to act so reck-
lessly. She was angry with Dean, too.

The June trip to Cancun had been a celebration of Sami
getting her master's in education, their twenty-fifth wedding
anniversary and of finally getting out of debt. They were
happy, and had enjoyed their time with the girls. Claire had
forgotten to pack her diaphragm so Dean had bought
condoms. They'd laughed about it, feeling young. Evidently it hadn't worked—as it hadn't twenty-five years ago.

The heat became unbearable so she strolled back to the
house, where the air-conditioning cooled her heated emotions. After getting bottled water out of the refrigerator, she
went into the bedroom and fished the letters out of her bag.
Curling up on the sofa, she untied the worn ribbon and felt
as if she was opening a part of her soul.

For a moment she just stared at the letters and wondered
why they were so important to her. Every time she and
Dean had moved, she'd tucked the letters in a safe spot.
Why?

She wasn't sure. Maybe it was because they depicted her
dedication, her love and her accomplishments as a woman,
as a wife and as a mother. Or maybe deep down she knew
one day she would need them for guidance and inspiration.

For twenty-five years she'd tried to be the perfect wife
and mother. When Sami started school, Claire became a
teacher's aide so she would be close in case the girls
needed her. The family had also needed the money.

When she was growing up, her father had wanted her
to follow in his footsteps and become a lawyer. That plan
was derailed when she became pregnant in high school.
But as Claire worked in the school system, her goal had

changed. She loved working with kids, mostly the young ones, whose minds were waiting to unfurl with just the right incentives and the guidance of a caring teacher.

As those thoughts ran through her mind, Claire realized she'd forgotten about plans with two friends, Nita and Joan, for tomorrow. They were going to a spa for the works, to celebrate Claire's return to college full-time. Then they were meeting the guys for dinner.

She reached for her cell, but just fiddled with it, unsure of what to say. "Guess what? I'm pregnant." Even though her friends would understand, she wasn't up to saying those words yet. When she was stronger, she'd call and cancel.

So many times she'd tried to go to college to get her degree, so she could teach instead of being an aide, but life's crises kept getting in the way. Now that their youngest daughter had graduated, Claire was ready to embark on her own career, fulfill her dream.

But now...

She slipped a finger beneath the flap of an envelope. What had her life been about? What had kept her from getting her degree before now? As she unfolded a letter, her body trembled with old fears. Each page was filled with *I love you's* and plans for the future. Wonderful plans that only a teenager could believe.

Jan 9, 1983

My darling Dean,

I haven't seen you in two days and I feel alone, so I close my eyes and I can see you. Your dark hair curls into your collar and I remember the texture, the feel of it against my fingers. And I see your smile, that lazy grin that makes me warm all over. But your eyes are what comfort me. Those soft, caring blue eyes that tease me, tempt me and make me a little crazy. I love you so much...

In a trancelike state, she glanced through the floor-to-ceiling windows to the view of the lake. Her parents had forbidden her to see Dean. He wasn't the type of boy she should be dating. His mother was a waitress and not up to the Thornton standards for friends and acquaintances. Dean had no future. He was a football jock who would be washed up before his time. Claire deserved better, her father had said, and though she might not agree then, she would thank him later.

As a teenager, those words hadn't meant much to her. All she knew was how Dean made her feel. Ever since third grade she thought he was wonderful, even when he untied her bows. In junior high they'd become an item, and that had never changed all through high school.

They couldn't date, but found ways to be together, especially after they started driving. Most of the time they talked, laughed and made out like other teenagers. In their senior year their emotions became heated and they gave in to temptation.

The first time was in Dean's car after a dance. Claire cried and so did he, but it had been the most beautiful experience of her life. She and Dean were now part of each other and nothing could keep them apart.

In the weeks that followed they stole moments after football games, met in the park, after school and on weekends at their secret place—Dean's house while his mother worked. It didn't matter that they were sneaking around. They were together, that was all that was important. Until...

She'd missed her period and she was nervous. They'd been so careful. Another week and she knew she had to tell Dean.

March 10, 1983

CLAIRE HUNG AROUND the gym, trying not to bite her nails as she waited for basketball practice to end and then waited again while Dean showered and changed clothes. He came out of the locker room smiling, and all she wanted to do was kiss him.

"Hey. I didn't expect to see you tonight," he said, walking toward her with his easy swagger in his letterman jacket and jeans.

"I have to talk to you." She couldn't keep the panic out of her voice.

He took her arm and led her out of the gym to the parking lot. "What is it? Did your parents find out?"

She shook her head.

A couple of guys from the team came out and waved to them.

Dean pulled her close to his side. His masculine scent mingling with fresh soap did a number on her senses. "Well, then, everything's okay. Let's go some place where it's quieter."

With self-control she pushed away. "No. We've done too much of that."

He frowned. "What? Make love?"

"Yes." She looked directly at him in the glow of the parking lot lights.

"Claire." He tried to take her in his arms and she stepped back.

"I'm pregnant."

There was total silence. A car honked and a girl's laughter carried on the wind.

He frowned. *"What?"*

"I missed my period and I know I'm pregnant. What are we going to do?"

"But how? We've used protection every time, and it's been hell getting condoms. Jarrod's older brother buys them and he charges me double. But at least I don't have to go into a store to get them."

"Evidently sometimes condoms don't work."

"God." He ran a hand through his hair. "This can't be happening."

"I know. We had it all planned. You're going to the University of Texas on a football scholarship and I'm enrolling there, too. We were finally going to be together without sneaking around."

He sucked in a deep breath. "Okay. We're both eighteen, so we'll get married and continue with our plans."

"On what? When my parents find out I'm pregnant, they'll disown me. They don't even know I've been seeing you."

"Then we'll make it on our own."

"Dean, be realistic. We'll have a child to raise and we'll both have to find jobs."

He slipped his arms around her and held her close. "Don't panic. Whatever happens, I'll be here for you and the baby. I'm not running out on you like my dad ran out on my mom and me. First, make an appointment with the doctor and let's find out for sure."

She trailed her hands to the strong column of his neck, needing to touch his skin. She kissed his ear, his jaw, and felt his muscles tighten.

"I love you," she whispered.

Cupping her face with both hands, he ran his tongue over her lips. "I love you, too. And we'll face this together. If you're pregnant, we'll have to tell your parents."

She winced. "It's going to be an ugly scene."

"Yeah." He kissed her deeply and she clung to him.

The March wind blew against them, but they kept holding on to each other. Holding on to the now, the present, their love. In the days to come their love would be tested, and neither knew if it would survive the pressures of the outside world.

CHAPTER TWO

A Week Later...

THEY SAT IN THE DOCTOR'S office waiting for the result of the pregnancy test. Dean had skipped basketball practice, and Claire loved him all the more for that. She couldn't face this alone.

The nurse called them into a small room and they waited some more.

"Are you nervous?" Dean asked, clutching Claire's hand.

"A little."

"Me, too."

The doctor came in with a folder and sat at his desk.

"Dr. Miller, this is Dean Rennels, my boyfriend."

"Nice to meet you, son." They shook hands. "I've seen you play football. Very impressive."

"Thank you, sir."

"I'm glad you're with Claire today." He glanced at the contents in the folder. "The test is positive. You're pregnant—about two months. The baby should be born in late September."

Her heart fell to the pit of her stomach and for a moment she couldn't breathe. Dean turned a sickly white. The silence told its own story—two young people caught between love and reality, without a clue as to the difference.

Dr. Miller closed the folder. "I can see this is a shock. I always tell women they have three choices—abortion, adoption or acceptance. It's your decision, Claire."

Abortion! She couldn't kill their baby. Nor could she give it up for adoption. That left acceptance. She swallowed hard, words congealing with the bile in her throat.

Dean stood. "We're getting married, sir."

"I see." Dr. Miller looked at Claire. "Do your parents know this?"

"No, and I'd appreciate it if you wouldn't mention it until I do."

The doctor fidgeted. "My wife was here the day you came in for the test. When she saw your mom at the club, she casually mentioned she'd seen you. Dorian spoke out of turn and I'm sorry for that. I would never divulge your situation."

"How could she?" The Millers and her parents belonged to the same country club. Claire had seen the doctor's wife that day and never dreamed she'd say anything to her mother. That was three days ago and her mom hadn't said a word. Why?

"Dorian just thought you were in for a checkup. I'm so sorry."

Claire rose on shaky legs. "It doesn't matter. It's not going to remain a secret long."

Once they were in the hall, she was shaking so violently that Dean pulled her into a small waiting area to sit down.

"Are you okay?"

She had to take several deep breaths. "What are we going to do?"

"Get married like we planned."

"What about college?"

"We'll manage." He rubbed her arm and his touch instilled a sense of calm in her. "We'll take one day at a time. I'll get a marriage license as soon as possible."

She blinked back a tear. Her parents had such dreams for their only child's wedding. Through tears she looked at him. "If I didn't love you so much, I'd hate you."

He winced. "I'm sorry. I didn't plan this, either."

"I know."

"I'm glad we're keeping the baby," he murmured.

"Could you live with yourself if we did anything different?"

"No." His eyes caught hers. "We love each other. We'll make it."

"Do you believe love is enough?"

He nodded. "Yes."

"Then I do, too."

She placed her hand in his, along with her heart and her life. Together they walked out of the building. At her car he kissed her, and she knew they were going to be okay. Then out of the corner of her eye she saw her dad's Lincoln.

"Oh my God."

"What?"

"There's my dad."

The car screeched to a stop a few feet from them. Both her parents got out.

"Get away from my daughter," Robert Thornton shouted at Dean, his face red with anger.

Dean didn't budge. "Claire and I are getting married."

"Like hell." Robert loosened his tie and jerked it off.

"Dad, please," Claire begged. "We're in love and…and I'm pregnant."

Her mother, Gwen, gasped.

"You bastard. I'll kill you for this." Robert took a step toward Dean, but Gwen caught his arm. "Robert, watch your temper."

Her father sucked in a breath. "Get in the car, Claire."

"Dad…"

"Get in the car or I'm calling the cops and having this bastard arrested. Your choice."

"Please, Claire, let's go home," her mother pleaded.

There was nothing Claire could do. For now she had to follow her parents' instructions. She looked back at Dean's shattered expression and her heart broke. Would she ever see him again?

In the Thornton Home…

CLAIRE SAT LISTENING to everything she'd done wrong. A numbness settled over her body—a numbness of her spirit and her soul.

She wanted Dean.

She needed Dean.

"How could you, Claire? How could you do this?" her mother asked. "You have your whole life ahead of you and now…" Gwen shook back her blond hair. "I'm just appalled at your blatant disobedience. That boy has been a bad influence on you. You never disobeyed us before you met him."

"I love him."

"At your age you don't even know what love is." Gwen's voice rose in anger. "I don't understand how you can be so smart and yet so dumb."

Before she could respond, her father came back into the room. "It's all set for first thing in the morning."

"What's all set?" Claire asked.

"I've made arrangements to have the baby aborted."

She felt the blood drain from her face. "No!" she screamed.

"It's for the best," her mother said. "You can't let this ruin your whole life. College is waiting for you. Later you can have all the children you want, and the wedding you've dreamed about. You'll thank us then."

Claire bit her lip to keep from screaming again and realized there was no point in talking to them. Their minds were made up. Slowly, she trudged upstairs. She curled up on her bed and cried for being so young and stupid.

And she cried for being in love.

After there were no tears left, she rallied her strength. No one was taking this baby from her. She phoned Dean.

"Claire, are you okay?"

"No. I have to get out of here. My father has made an appointment for an abortion in the morning."

"I'll be right there."

"No. After they're asleep, I'll call you."

"Okay."

"But where will I go?"

"You can stay here with Mom and me. She might be a little ticked off, but she won't kick us out."

"Are you sure?"

"Oh, yeah. I know my mom."

"Dean, I'm scared."

"Me, too."

"I love you."

"I love you, too."

She hung up and reached for pad and pen and wrote

Dean a letter, telling him how much she loved him. Putting her fears in writing helped to pass the time.

DEAN WAS WORRIED about Claire—it wasn't like her to go somewhere without telling him. And why had she taken the letters? As he sat in the den, his mind went back to that first night she'd left home.

March 16, 1983

DEAN PICKED UP CLAIRE right before midnight on the corner of her street. They didn't talk much. Neither knew if they were doing the right thing.

They made it to Bunny's before she got home from work. Her shift ended at twelve. When he told his mother what had happened, she exploded, just as he knew she would.

"We're planning on getting married," he told her.

"And that's supposed to solve everything." In her black-and-white uniform, a pencil behind one ear, Bunny glared at him, her hands on her hips. "I thought I raised you better than this. Protection! I've drilled that into your head since you were fourteen years old."

"We used protection, but it didn't work. I love Claire and she loves me. I'm getting a marriage license tomorrow. We just need a place to stay."

Bunny threw up her hands. "Champ, do you think it's that easy? The Thorntons will be knocking down my door as soon as they discover Claire's gone."

"I'm not going back," Claire said. "They want me to have an abortion."

"What?" Bunny's face turned almost as red as her hair.

"We can't let that happen, Mom. Please help us."

She rubbed the balls of her hands into her eyes. "Champ, that's why I have to dye my hair. You've turned it almost completely white."

"Then you'll let us stay here?"

"Yes." She pointed a red-tipped finger at Claire. "But you're sleeping on the sofa."

"She can have my bed."

"Then *you're* sleeping on the sofa."

"Don't you think it's a little late for that?"

"Those are the rules, champ. And you had better prepare yourself for fireworks in the morning."

Dean didn't argue with Bunny. He was glad he and Claire could be together, or at least in the same place. He sat with her for a while and left her reading. Her suitcase was full of books, some of her favorites—Shakespeare, Dickens, Brontë, Austen, Alcott and many more.

Tossing and turning, he couldn't get comfortable. It wasn't the lumpy sofa, though. Facing the Thorntons weighed heavily on his mind.

Early the next morning the pounding on the door woke them. "Police, open up."

Bunny came out of her room, her hair sticking out in all directions. "What the hell?"

Claire hurried out, still in her clothes. She hadn't undressed and neither had Dean. The beat of his heart sounded like a cymbal in his ears. He reached for her hand and she trembled.

Bunny opened the door.

"Good morning, ma'am," a police officer said. "I'm looking for Claire Thornton. Is she here?"

"Yes. I'm here," Claire answered.

Bunny stepped aside. The officer, followed by the Thorntons, entered the house.

"Let's go, Claire," Robert said.

Claire shook her head. "No. I'm not going with you."

"Yes, you are. The officer is here to see that you do."

"I'm eighteen and I can make my own decisions."

"Young lady," the policeman said. "Just get your things and let's go."

"I can't. They want me to have an abortion and I can't do that."

The officer looked at Robert.

"Do your damn job," he snapped.

"I can't force her. She's eighteen."

"I know the police chief."

"Well, then, you better call him. I was under the impression the young lady was here against her will."

"She is," Gwen said. "She doesn't know what she's doing."

"She seems fine to me."

"Claire, come home. Please," her mother pleaded. "If you insist on having the baby, we'll send you up north. It can be adopted by a nice couple."

Claire's nails dug into Dean's palm. "I'm keeping my baby."

"I'm getting tired of this defiance, Claire," Robert said, his face turning beet-red. "If you insist on this insanity, I wash my hands of you. Do you want your mother and me completely out of your life?"

Claire swallowed. "I know I've disappointed you. I'm sorry, but I can't change the way I feel. I'm having the baby."

"That's it," Robert said in anger. "If you're choosing

him—" he flung a hand toward Dean "—over us, then you're on your own. Don't call us for money or anything. You're no daughter of mine."

"Robert." Gwen grabbed his arm. "No."

"I said that's it. Let's go."

Gwen followed her husband and the officer out of the room. Claire whimpered deep in her throat. Dean held her tight as heartbroken sobs convulsed through her body. The sound tore at his gut like jagged glass. At that moment he grew up. He was eighteen years old and he was too young for fatherhood. He was too young for this kind of heartache. But he would shoulder it like a man.

DEAN DRAGGED HIS HANDS over his face. How he wished life had been easy after Claire had made that sacrifice, but it hadn't. She'd worked two jobs, as a clerk at a department store and at night for a fast-food place. He put in countless hours at a record store. They lived with Bunny until practice started for college football. He and Claire moved into college housing and finally had their own place.

Claire carried most of the financial load, since he couldn't play ball, work and go to school. There were times she didn't feel well and she still went to work. He felt like the biggest louse that had ever been born. One day, he would make her life better, but there'd been so many obstacles in the way then....

Dean walked into the kitchen. *Claire, where are you?* He reread the note. She needed to get away. Why? Where did she go when she wanted peace and quiet?

The lake house.

He grabbed his car keys.

CLAIRE SAT CROSS-LEGGED, the letters in her lap. She opened another.

My darling Dean,

I'm so afraid I'm going to have the baby while you're away on a road trip. I don't know if I can do this by myself, but I'll never tell you that. If the time comes and you're not here, I'll just close my eyes and picture your loving face, like I always do. I love you, and our baby is going to be perfect—just like you.

She closed her eyes and let herself relive a moment of that fear.

September 24, 1983

"YOU HAVEN'T TOLD DEAN, have you?" Bunny asked, stopping by the dorm to check on her. She always did that when Dean was away. Bunny, with her in-your-face attitude, was a hard person to get to know, but Claire had come to love her dearly.

Claire ran her hand over her protruding stomach. "No. I haven't told Dean I'm having contractions."

"He needs to be here."

"He has a scholarship to play football and he can't miss a game."

"He's also going to have a baby."

Claire heaved a sigh. "I have to go to work."

"What? You're having contractions. What are you thinking?"

Claire kissed her cheek. "I'm thinking you worry too much."

Bunny caught her arm. "Be reasonable…"

Claire held up a hand to stop her. "If the baby starts to come, the manager will call an ambulance."

"Oh, for crying out loud." Bunny stomped her foot. "Sometimes you love that son of mine too much!"

Smiling, Claire reached for her purse just as someone knocked at the door. Bunny quickly opened it. Gwen stood there.

"Mom." Claire hadn't seen her mother since the police tried to take her home. Robert had forbidden Gwen to contact her. Their plan was that Claire would see the error of her ways and return home. But it hadn't happened.

"May I speak with you, please?" her mom asked.

Claire looked past her and didn't see her father. That meant he didn't know Gwen had come. Tears stung the back of Claire's eyes. "I'm on my way to work," she said abruptly.

Gwen paled. "In your condition?"

"Yes. We need the money." She held up her head and forced the tears away.

Her mom reached into her purse and pulled out a wad of hundred dollar bills. "Take this. I'll bring more every week."

Claire backed away. "Sorry. I can't take your money. Dean and I are doing just fine."

"Oh, yeah." Gwen flung out a hand, the diamonds on her fingers sparkling. "He's off having the time of his life while you're here pregnant and working."

"Please leave."

"Claire, it's not too late. You can give up the child for adoption and go on with your life. Remember how we talked about you joining my old sorority and—"

"Do you really think I could carry this child for nine months and just give it away?"

"Claire…"

"Please leave—now." She was losing her temper and the tight rein she had on her emotions.

Gwen shoved the money at her. "Take it."

"No thanks. Dean and I are doing fine."

Her mother glanced around the small apartment. "I would hardly call this fine."

Bunny stepped around Claire. "You'd better leave before I plant my foot in your snobby mouth."

"How dare you?" Gwen spluttered.

"Mom, just leave," Claire said, knowing her mother-in-law was getting angry.

Gwen whirled away and left.

As Bunny closed the door, she said, "She's right, you know. You don't need to be working."

"Whose side are you on?" Claire slipped the strap of her purse over her shoulder and winced as a pain shot up her back.

"I don't think you have to ask that."

"No." Bunny was unwavering in her support.

She studied Claire for a moment. "Stay home until the baby comes, and I'll buy the groceries and pay the bills."

Claire lifted an eyebrow. "You'll work two shifts, right?"

"Done it before and I can do it again."

Claire hugged her. "Thanks. But we'll manage."

"You're so stubborn."

At the fast-food place, she continued to have contractions. At times they were so bad she couldn't concentrate. Her eyes were glued to the clock. The team was due to land at the airport at eleven. She couldn't have the baby until Dean arrived.

At ten forty-five she collapsed into a ball of pain, and the manager called an ambulance.

The next thing she knew they were at the hospital. "Mrs. Rennels, are you ready to have this baby?" the doctor asked.

"No." She hissed between contractions. "No. My husband's not here."

"I don't think the baby's going to wait."

Bunny came running in. The manager had phoned her. "How are you, sugar?"

"Dean. I need Dean." The words came out as a pathetic cry, but Claire couldn't help it.

"I just spoke to him. He's on his way from the airport."

"Okay." She could breathe normally now. Dean was coming.

A pain ripped through her abdomen, and it took all the strength she had not to push or scream or cry.

"Mrs. Rennels, it's time to push," the doctor said.

"I can't. My husband's not here. Please…" A wail erupted from her throat.

"Mrs. Rennels…"

Loud voices could be heard in the hall and then Dean came charging in. "Claire." He kissed her face over and over. "Thank God I made it. I was so afraid…"

Claire let out a long breath. "Me, too." She drew on her last ounce of strength. "Okay. I'm ready to have our baby."

Fifteen minutes later, Dean placed their baby daughter into her arms. A feeling of pride and love suffused her. But a part of her grieved that her parents weren't here to share this miracle. This precious gift.

"She's so tiny," she whispered weakly.

"And perfect," Dean said with pride. "Ten toes. Ten fingers. And the most precious little face. She looks just like you. Absolutely beautiful."

"You think so?"

"You bet. What are we going to name her?"

Claire studied the precious bundle in her arms. "How about Sarah Margaret? After Bunny. What do you think?"

"Oh, honey. Mom will be so excited. It's perfect."

"Yes…"

Fatigue overwhelmed Claire and her eyes drooped, but in that instant, with her baby in her arms and Dean smiling at her, she knew she'd made the right choice.

CHAPTER THREE

As Dean drove toward Lake Travis, the bright Texas sun dimmed to twilight gray. Darkness would soon blanket the hills and Claire still hadn't called. If she couldn't get him at home, she'd try his cell. But so far nothing. He knew something was really wrong.

For once everything was right in their world. Both their daughters were on their own. Their youngest, Sami, already had a job at a school in the nearby town of Round Rock. Both girls had received the education Claire and Dean had wanted for them. And now Claire had the time he'd always wanted for her—time for herself—to earn that college degree.

Ten days and her dream would start becoming a reality. His own college days had been one big guilt trip. He'd been away at games, traveling, while Claire was at home working and taking care of a new baby.

It wasn't long after Sarah was born that they noticed the wheezing. She was also phlegmy, with a constant cold and cough. At times she didn't want to nurse. Claire was continually in the doctor's office with her. The pediatrician kept her on antibiotics, and they worried about their baby taking so much medication.

Then the ear infections started, and Sarah was hospitalized twice for pneumonia. Claire got very little sleep because the baby needed lots of attention. That made her load heavier, but she'd never complained. Several nights Dean found her in the rocker, crying and holding Sarah. Claire was worried something was really wrong with their child and the doctors couldn't find it. Dean was worried, too. He would sit and hold both of them until the morning light. That was all he could do, and at times he felt so helpless.

The first few months, Claire couldn't work, and lost her jobs. His mother helped, and Dean tried to take care of Sarah at night. But Claire always seemed to be awake.

At times it was a struggle for Sarah to breathe. Claire did tons of research and insisted on a diagnosis. The doctor suspected she had asthma, but said Sarah was too little for him to know for sure. He said her airways were inflamed, and would heal with antibiotics and time.

That wasn't good enough for Claire and Dean, and they immediately switched doctors. Sarah was put on a nebulizer machine for albuterol treatments. It plugged into the wall and had tubing and a mask that went over her nose and mouth. The medication went into the machine and Sarah breathed it in. They saw results almost immediately.

The new doctor agreed that Sarah had asthma, and said that some children grow out of it. But at least their baby was getting better. Dean and Claire were so relieved.

It was a hard time, however. Sarah also had allergies, and Claire washed her bedding every day to get rid of dust mites. They covered the mattress and pillows with allergy covers and gave away all her stuffed toys. Bunny bought a humidifier because they couldn't afford to.

Once they adjusted to Sarah and her needs, life settled down. Claire started tutoring students so she could stay at home. The pay was very good and it worked out well.

Dean had heard it said that you can't live on love, but during those first few years they had very little else.

CLAIRE STARED AT THE phone, wanting to call Dean. She needed to hear his voice, but she wasn't ready to tell him yet. She had to continue to examine her life alone—to measure the sacrifices she'd made. Were they sacrifices or was that what love was?

She opened a letter—one she'd written while waiting for Dean to come home from a football game, a time she'd questioned that sacrifice.

Dean,
Sarah had one of those days. Nothing seems to help her breathing and she's fussy. I feel so helpless...

The page blurred.

November 12, 1983

SARAH WAS SIX WEEKS OLD and Claire had been up with her most of the night. She was exhausted, her nerves frayed. She curled up in a rocker, trying to get Sarah to nurse, but the baby kept spitting out the nipple. Claire worried she wasn't getting enough milk.

Texas was playing football and Claire flipped on the TV to watch her husband. Bunny came by to catch the game with her, and made popcorn. Claire was glad to have her company.

Just as Sarah went to sleep, Bunny yelled at the TV and the baby woke up.

"Sugar, I'm sorry. I get all excited when I see my boy getting bruised."

"It's okay." Claire stood. "I'll put her in her bed and maybe she'll sleep for a while."

"Why don't you lie down, too, sugar?" Bunny suggested.

"Are you kidding? I want to watch Dean so I'll know what he's talking about when he tells me about the game."

Sarah went to sleep quickly, and Claire hurried back to the living room. The game was tied, with less than ten seconds to play. The two women sat on the edge of their seats, biting their nails. Texas had the ball. The quarterback threw a long pass, and Claire and Bunny jumped to their feet, holding their breath as the pigskin sailed through the air. Dean leaped high in the end zone and dragged it in with the tips of his fingers. The fans went crazy and Claire and Bunny hugged, careful not to shout too loudly.

With the game over, fans poured onto the field. A reporter held a mike out to Dean and asked him a couple of questions. The noisy crowd prevented Claire from hearing him clearly, but she saw his smile—that lazy grin that turned her knees to pure sweet honey.

His sweaty hair hung across his forehead and he reached up to touch it, a signal to Claire that he was thinking about her. Smiling, she tugged her hair in response. The camera followed Dean as he jogged toward the locker room. A blonde grabbed him and kissed him. The reporter commented he hoped that was Dean's wife.

But it wasn't.

Claire sank into her chair, her joy dissipating. For the first time, she realized other women saw Dean as an attractive man, just as she did. The understanding left her in a state of shock. She should be there with him, sharing these moments of victory in his life. Instead she was home, feeling very left out.

Bunny caught the look on her face. "Sugar, don't pay that any attention. It means nothing to Dean."

For the first time, Claire wondered about that, too. "I don't know, Bunny. I'm tired most of the time. Sarah spits up all over me and I smell like spoiled milk. I don't feel very attractive."

"Now you just stop thinking like that right now, do you hear me? Dean loves you and that little girl in there."

"But don't you think he's flattered by the attention?"

"He's a man, sugar. Of course he is, but I know my boy. His one thought now is to get back to you and Sarah."

Claire wasn't so sure. Life just seemed to be one jolt after another, and she didn't know how much longer she could hold it together. Could her parents have been right? Was she too young to even know what true love was all about? No. She would never believe that. Not for one instant.

That night she lay in bed waiting for Dean. The game was out of town, so she knew it would be late when he came home.

She was half-asleep when she heard his key in the lock. A few minutes later, he slipped into bed beside her.

"Hey, beautiful."

She wiggled in his arms. "I don't feel beautiful."

"What?" He turned on the bedside lamp. "What's wrong?"

Pushing her hair out of her eyes, she sat up. "I saw you kissing that girl." Claire hated that she couldn't keep the hurt out of her voice.

He caressed her cheek and she leaned her face into his hand, loving his gentle touch. "I didn't kiss her. She kissed me, and I have no idea who she was."

"Still…"

He reached for something on the nightstand. "I wrote this on the plane."

Unfolding the paper, she read,

My sweet Claire,
Today I realized why I'm hooked on your kisses.
They're sweeter than watermelon wine and hotter than
a hooker's on Saturday night. No other woman can
ever top that.

A bubble of laughter left her throat. "We've both had
Bunny's watermelon wine, but how do you know what a
hooker's kiss tastes like?"

He grinned. "Purely a guess."

"Now I know why you made such awful grades in
English."

He gently laid her down. "There's only one woman I
want to kiss." His lips trailed a line of fire from her neck
to her jaw. When his mouth covered hers, any remaining
doubts vanished. All she felt was happiness.

Looking into her eyes, he said, "I love you. Only you."

She ran her fingers through his hair. "You better. We
have a baby to raise."

He glanced at the crib. "I see she's sleeping."

"Yes, finally."

"Tomorrow I'll watch her and you can rest." He rolled
onto Claire. "But now we need some fun time."

As he turned out the light she giggled like a schoolgirl.
He wanted her. That's what she needed to hear—to know.
It was important to her as a woman.

But her faith in their love was tested once more.

When Sarah was six months old, Claire discovered she
was pregnant again. She was on the pill, but something had
gone wrong. Being up with Sarah so much, she was ex-

hausted most of the time, and obviously had forgotten to take it. She cursed herself. She cursed Dean.

"God, this can't be happening again," he said when she told him.

"Well, it is. I can't do this. I can't handle two babies by myself. You're gone all the time and I'm stuck here."

She couldn't believe the words coming out of her mouth. She'd never dreamed she felt that way. But she did.

"I help, too."

"Your mother helps. Most nights you're out having fun." Emotions too long bottled up came spilling out.

"Claire, that's not fair."

"No, it isn't," she screamed. "I'm the one making all the sacrifices. I'm the one…" Anger consumed her and she tore out of the apartment.

"Claire," Dean called, but she kept running.

She stopped in a small park on campus to catch her breath. Her head pounded with doubts, insecurities and with the reality of growing up. As an adult, wasn't she supposed to be wiser? And wasn't she supposed to have learned from her mistakes?

Sinking onto the grass, she wrapped her arms around her legs and watched as couples strolled hand in hand, oblivious to everything but each other. She and Dean had been like that, so much in love. Life and responsibilities were suddenly too much.

As Dean walked toward her, she scrambled to her feet. "Where's Sarah?" she asked.

"Mom's with her."

"You always do that—call Bunny. Sarah is your responsibility, not your mother's."

He frowned. "I had to find you."

Claire whirled away. "I can't do this. I can't have another baby. As soon as Sarah was better, I was planning to enroll for classes. Now…"

"What are you saying?"

She faced him. "I'm exhausted physically and emotionally. I…"

"I'm sorry you're pregnant." For the first time he seemed angry. "But you're the one who forgot to take the pill."

"Why is that my responsibility?"

He jammed both hands through his hair. "I don't know. It just is."

"Well, it shouldn't be, because I'm lousy at it."

His mouth twitched. "Honey…" He reached for her.

She backed away. "Don't touch me. I can't think when you do that."

"What do you want me to do?"

"I don't know." She paused, her voice dropping to barely a whisper. "I just want to feel happy again."

"Claire, honey." He wrapped his arms around her and she sagged against him. "I'm sorry life has been so hard."

"I know." She looked into his blue eyes. "Undo my bow."

"What?"

"Undo my bow."

Frowning, he yanked the ribbon that held back her blond hair, and it tumbled to her shoulders. She spun and took off running across the grass, her hair flying behind her. He caught her in less than ten seconds. Laughing, they whirled around as a light rain began to fall. They hardly noticed as they slowly began to dance, locked in each other's arms. Raindrops pelted their heads, but they didn't mind. They were young and in love and remembering how wonderful that felt.

"I love it when we dance—even without music," he said, kissing her face.

The scent of rain mingled with the smell of him, and her heart brimmed with happiness. She'd lost it for a moment. "Me, too. I love you."

He stopped moving and cupped her face, his thumbs making wet circles on her cheeks. "I love you with all my heart."

She smiled, blinking in the rain. "We're having another baby," she whispered, feeling his love—the love that made her happy and complete.

"Yes." He kissed her softly. "You okay?"

"I am now." She took his hand. "Let's go home."

DEAN DROVE UP to the lake house and saw Claire's car. She was here. The heat of the day had subsided and a sticky warmth prevailed. But it was fresh, not contaminated with gas fumes or other foul city emissions.

He could barely see the house in the darkness, but he knew exactly what it looked like—brown cedar Hardiplanks with a wood deck on the front and the back. The interior was small, with two bedrooms, one bath and a combination kitchen and large den that overlooked the lake.

It had taken every resource they had to swing buying the place. Claire had made another sacrifice. She'd put off going to college so they could afford two house payments. He didn't want her to, but Claire had insisted. That's the way she was—always putting her family first.

The girls loved it here, but he wondered how often they'd come back now. Sarah was very studious, like her mother. She was doing an internship in law. Soon she'd take the bar. Samantha was more like him—an athlete.

Tennis was her sport, and she was very good, an ace player in high school and college. She would now be teaching physical education and coaching tennis.

Memories swirled around him. He'd wanted to give Claire the world, but he'd busted up his leg in his senior year, and although it had healed, he knew he had to think about her and the girls. He had to be home for them, so he forgot his dream of playing pro football and took a job teaching and coaching.

He was now the head coach and athletic director at a high school. The last four years he'd been building a great team, and if everything fell into place as he'd planned, they were going to win the state championship again this year. Football was in his blood and probably always would be.

Just as Claire was.

Through the window, he could see her sitting on the sofa, the letters strewn around her. At forty-three she still looked beautiful, a gorgeous blonde with soft brown eyes. She had a kind heart and a sweet nature. That's probably what he loved most about her. And she made him feel young, powerful and all male. Her breasts were fuller now, as were her hips, and she could still heat him up just as quickly as she had back then.

Back then...they'd been through so much. But in truth Claire had been through so much more than him.

December 26, 1984

CHRISTMAS WAS MEAGER at their house. He'd given Claire earrings and she'd bought him a pullover sweater. They'd spent the day at Bunny's. Sarah was struggling to breathe and wanted only Claire to hold her. Dean took care of Sami, but he couldn't nurse her, so he had to hand the baby to her, too. Claire was exhausted and he became more aware of that than ever, maybe because he was with them the whole day.

The next day he started practice for the upcoming bowl game. That evening when he came home, Claire was sitting on the living room floor nursing Sami in one arm while Sarah nestled into her side with a breathing mask over her nose and mouth, taking a treatment. Claire's hair hung limply around her shoulders, sour milk stained her blouse and she looked as tired as he'd ever seen her.

He quickly sank down by her and took Sarah and finished the treatment. As he held his little girl, patting her back, she went to sleep. He carried her into their bedroom and laid her in her crib.

The apartment was cramped, with one bedroom, a living area and kitchen combination, and a small bathroom. He and Claire had a crib on each side of their bed, and that was a problem. She wasn't getting any sleep.

As he returned to the living room, he saw Sami was through nursing. He scooped her out of her mother's arms and burped her.

Claire's head fell back against the cushions. "I'm so tired," she murmured.

Dean carried Sami to her crib and within minutes she was asleep. After partially closing the door, he went back to Claire. He gathered her into his arms and placed her on the sofa.

Kissing her gently, he said, "Just go to sleep, honey." He reached for an afghan and covered her.

She snuggled into the cushions. "Don't let me sleep too long."

"I won't."

He turned off the lights and watched her for a moment

before he made his way to the bedroom and closed the door. Both babies awoke during the night. He changed them, and gave Sarah a bottle after which she went back to sleep. But Sami was different. He carried her to Claire, who nursed her without really waking up.

Early the next morning he got up, made breakfast, then took it to Claire on a tray.

She stirred, glanced around and quickly sat up. "Where are the girls?"

"Asleep."

She yawned. "What time is it?"

"About six."

Her eyes went wide. "You let me sleep all night?"

"Yep. And here's breakfast." He pointed to the tray. "Scrambled eggs, toast and your favorite orange marmalade."

"Oh, my. I feel like a queen."

He sat beside her and took her into his arms. "You're my queen."

She rested her head on his shoulder. "You have practice today and I know you had to get up with the girls."

"I can go on very little sleep." He kissed the side of her face. "Football season will be over in a week, and classes won't start for a couple more weeks. I'll be here to help out more."

"Thank you. I love you."

He just held her and stared at the small Christmas tree they'd positioned on an end table. They had to put it up high because Sarah was walking and she'd pull it over in no time. Claire had decorated it with red bows and shiny balls, along with their special first Christmas ornament and this year's new ornament. It wasn't much, but it was all they had. Staring at the sparse tree, he vowed one day he would give her everything.

But "one day" always seemed to be out of his reach.

DEAN CONTINUED TO WATCH Claire through the window, and as he did, a frisson of fear shot through him. Why was she reading the letters? Could it just be nerves? Or was it something more? Suddenly he had to know.

He opened the door and stepped in.

"DEAN." Claire wasn't expecting him, and for a moment she was speechless.

"I was worried about you." He moved some letters and sat beside her, kissing her cheek. "Feeling better?"

"Mmm. How did you know where to find me?"

"A lucky guess." He tucked her hair behind her ear and her heart contracted. He was so handsome. Threads of gray shone in his dark hair and his features were leaner, more mature. She loved him so much, but how were they going to get through this? How was she going to tell him?

"You didn't have to come. I'm fine. I just needed some fresh air." It was the first time she'd lied to him.

"Do you think you have the flu?"

"I'm not sure." She bit her lip to keep from telling another lie. "Did you get Bunny settled?"

"Yes. She's all moved in."

"She should be living with us. We have room." When Dean had gotten a job teaching, they'd bought their first house. Claire loved the older homes on the tree-lined boulevards in the old Tarrytown area near the heart of central Austin, so they'd bought a two-story Victorian that had been built in the early 1900s. After they renovated, it was the perfect home, roomy and with lots of character. They still lived there.

Dean shrugged. "You know how Mom is. She likes her independence. And she said we need some time alone. We've never had that."

"Mmm." Claire glanced at the letters, feeling her chest close up. It wasn't going to happen now, either. How did she tell him that once again she'd screwed up? Although she wasn't sure why she was blaming herself. Dean was involved, too.

He followed her glance. "Why are you reading the letters?"

She swallowed. "To remember—the good and the bad. To remember dreams that don't come true."

"Claire, your dream *is* coming true."

"I…" Her throat locked because of what she had to say.

"I know you're nervous about college, about attending classes with students younger than your daughters. You'll be fine, though."

"Don't try to pacify me." The words came out angry, though she didn't mean them to.

There was silence—a strained silence, which was rare. They could always talk about anything. But now…

Dean pulled her into his arms and she snuggled against him. "What's going on, Claire? Why did you just leave like that?"

"I wanted some time to think. That's all." Lazily, she drew circles on his T-shirt. She had to tell him.

"About what?"

She drew back and slowly raised her eyes to his. "I'm pregnant."

There was a noticeable pause.

"Excuse me?"

"I'm pregnant."

He gave a fake laugh. "No. No way."

"Really?" She lifted an eyebrow. "Remember Cancun and I forgot my diaphragm so we used a condom? Guess what? It didn't work—*again.*"

He sprang to his feet. "It's just nerves. You can't be pregnant."

She held up the letters. "I remember thinking that twice before."

"I refuse to believe it. You've been on an emotional high getting ready for college. That's all it is."

"I know when I'm pregnant."

"Have you seen a doctor?"

"No."

"Well, then…"

"You can keep batting excuses through the air, but it's not going to change a thing. I'm pregnant."

As the words finally sank in, he closed his eyes as if he was in pain. "Oh, God, not again. Not now."

"That's why I wanted this time alone, to think about what to do."

His eyes flew open. "What do you mean?"

"I have choices."

"You mean…"

"I don't know what I mean. I'm trying to accept this, trying to let go of that foolish college dream. But right now I'm stuck in anger mode. This time I want to take the easy way out and I can't even believe…"

"What can't you believe?"

She licked her dry lips, knowing she had to tell him what she'd done. "This morning when I realized what was wrong with me, I bought a pregnancy test. It confirmed what I suspected." She swallowed. "Then I…I drove to the Planned Parenthood Clinic. I'm a woman. I have rights. And I wasn't letting my dream slip away again. All I could think about was myself."

"And?"

"I sat in the car praying for strength, and suddenly it felt like God slapped me in the face. I was thinking about killing our baby without even talking to you. I can't believe I did such a thing."

"Claire, honey." He moved toward her.

"No. Don't come near me or I might strangle you."

He paled.

"I'm sorry. I have to sort through everything I'm feeling…alone."

"But you're not in this alone. It's my child, too."

She looked directly at him. "Yes, but your forty-three-year-old body will not be giving birth. Your dream will not be snatched from you again."

"You can still go to college and be pregnant. A woman can do it all."

"I don't want someone else raising my child."

"I'll help."

"Football practice has already started and your time at home is limited. That limits your help, too. And you're hoping to get a college coaching job."

"I'll turn it down."

She groaned. "Oh, yeah, guilt is just what I need."

"Claire…"

"I'm the mother. I'm the one who will do all the work, the one to make all the sacrifices."

"I made sacrifices, too. I gave up a pro football career."

"You didn't give it up. You injured your knee."

"I still had offers."

"What?" The color drained from her face. "You weren't taken in the draft and you never mentioned any offers."

"Because I knew it was time for me to be at home for you and the girls."

Her eyes narrowed. "You kept it from me? Did you think I was so weak that I couldn't take the news?"

"You're the strongest woman I know and it was so long ago I don't know why we're talking about it."

"Because you kept it from me as if I was some dependent, fragile wife who needed you at home."

"Claire, I turned it down for two reasons." He held up one finger. "I wanted to be home." He held up another finger. "Because of my injury I would have been second string, and that wasn't acceptable to me."

She glanced down at her hands, some of her anger leaving her. "That must have hurt."

"Not really. I had to put my family first." He took another step toward her. "Honey, we can work this out."

"Probably," she said. "But I need some time to accept the pregnancy graciously and with love—the same deep love with which I accepted Sarah and Sami." She wasn't sure why she was fighting for time or why she was arguing with Dean. Maybe she blamed him. She needed to come to terms with that, too.

"So what are you actually saying?"

"I'm saying you go home and I'll stay here."

He paled even more. "You want us to separate?"

"Yes. For now. College starts in ten days and by then I'll know if I'm going to go or not."

"I don't understand why you're shutting me out."

"I don't either. All I know is that I have to keep remembering, reading the letters to experience that deep well of commitment and love I had then. I have to let go of the dream with dignity and not blame it on a precious, innocent baby." She blinked back a tear. "We'll be in our sixties when this child graduates from high school. Can you handle that? I'm not sure I can."

"Claire…"

"I'm just being honest, and I hate myself for the selfish things I'm thinking. At this moment I hate everything."

He swallowed visibly. "Do you hate me?"

She looked at him. "I've loved you forever. I love your smile, your kind heart, your compassion and caring, even the gray in your hair. I love everything about you, but I'm not feeling any of that love right now."

"You will. The Claire I love can deal with anything."

"Maybe this is the one thing she can't."

"I'll never believe that."

"Dean." She sighed. "Go home and let me sort through this."

"We've never been apart."

"Yes, we have. It just never felt like it."

He blew out a hard breath. "I don't guess I have a choice."

"No."

He pointed to the letters. "Read every one of those and you'll feel our love again. We can overcome anything, even having a child at our age." He leaned over and kissed her lips. She breathed in his scent and forced herself not to respond.

"I love you," he whispered. "I'll call tomorrow."

"No, don't. I'll phone when I'm ready to talk."

His eyes darkened, but he didn't say anything.

"Dean," she called as he turned away. He quickly glanced at her. "Please cancel our plans for tomorrow."

"Oh."

"Tell Nita and Joan I'll call them later." She was passing the buck, but she couldn't handle a conversation with anyone.

He nodded. "I'll take care of it." Slowly, he walked out of the lake house.

She wanted to call him back, but that wouldn't solve anything. As the door closed, she knew their lives were changing, and she didn't feel it was for the better.

They loved each other. There was no doubt in her mind about that. To save her marriage she had to feel that forever kind of love she'd felt at eighteen.

How did she do that when she felt empty, afraid and lost within herself? There was only one thing she knew to do.

She picked up a letter.

CHAPTER FOUR

November 26, 1986

BUNNY INSISTED on watching the girls so Claire could make one of the home games. She sat in the stadium, her eyes on her husband. To her he was the best player on the field. She stood and cheered when he caught the ball. She bit her nails when it seemed to go right through his hands.

Suddenly a crashing tackle left him lying on the turf, writhing in pain, his leg bent at a strange angle. Jumping to her feet, she made her way to the field, her heart thumping so hard it was about to pound out of her chest.

As she reached the sidelines, an official stopped her.

"That's my husband," she cried, as the medical staff crowded around Dean.

"I'm sorry, ma'am, but—"

An ambulance backed into the stadium and she broke away. No one was keeping her away from him. Another official caught her before she reached him, but she jerked free, running to where Dean lay on a stretcher.

She fell to the turf by his side. "I'm here, honey."

"Claire—"

She stroked his face. "Shh."

The paramedics picked up the stretcher and she crawled

into the ambulance with him. No one tried to stop her. She rode to the hospital holding his hand. He was in a lot of pain and tried not to show it.

"Claire…"

"Hush. You'll be okay." But she wasn't so sure. His leg wasn't straight and had soon swollen to three times its normal size.

When they reached the hospital, things moved quickly. The doctor said Dean's kneecap was fractured in three places and his ligaments were torn. In a daze, she signed the papers for surgery.

Claire called to let Bunny know what had happened, but she already knew; she'd seen it on TV. Sarah had seen it, too, and was crying for her mommy and daddy. Claire re-assured her oldest daughter and then sat and waited, all alone, praying her husband was going to be fine.

The injury to his knee had looked bad. How was this going to affect his career, his hopes for the future? She didn't want his dream taken away from him. She knew how that felt.

She had to do something. Digging in her big bag, which Dean called her "monster purse," she found a pad she kept to jot down notes about Sarah and her asthma spells. She started to write…

My darling Dean,
Once again I feel alone and helpless. You have to be okay, and I'm praying with everything in me that you will be. I love you and I can't live without you…

Her tears fell onto the page and it took a moment before she could continue. One hour and a page full of I love you's later, the doctor came out. He shook her hand.

"Dean came through the surgery just fine. We had to replace his kneecap, and we repaired the torn ligaments, but I'm afraid he's out for the season. With therapy he might be able to bounce back and regain his speed. We'll just have to wait and see."

She felt a tightness in her chest. Dean had worked so hard and dreamed of the day a pro football career would put them on easy street. She worried how he was going to take the news.

"He's resting comfortably in recovery. You can see him soon."

The doctor walked away and Claire called Bunny. She had to talk to someone.

Later, she walked to Dean's room. Her heart contracted at the sight of her strong husband lying there, looking so pale.

"Hey, beautiful," he said in a drowsy voice.

Tears filled her eyes and she curled up in the bed beside him, on his good side. "How are you?"

He kissed her forehead. "I'm fine now."

"The doctor said—"

"You don't have to tell me. The football career is over. No team is going to want a wide receiver with a bad knee."

"I'm sorry."

He was so still, so silent, that she looked up. His eyes had filled with tears, and seeing them, she had trouble breathing.

"I wanted it for you, so you wouldn't have to work so hard. And I wanted you to go to college," he murmured.

"I will someday, when the girls start school." She kissed him and sat up. "Now we have to get you back on your feet."

"Claire—"

She placed a finger over his lips. "We'll get by like we always have." She picked up the phone on the nightstand.

"Now you have to say hi to our oldest daughter and let her know you're okay, and I'm sure Sami will want to babble some, too."

"Mom let them watch the game?"

"Yes."

"Damn."

"Dean..." Claire dialed the number and handed him the phone.

She listened to him chatting to the girls. With Sami, he did all the talking. Sami was nodding her head, Claire was sure. Dean was a great father, just as she'd known he would be. He would never let his daughters down.

Dean recovered quickly and attended the last game with the team, but he watched from the sidelines on crutches, and she was aware of how much that hurt him.

After the game, that night in bed, Dean was more aggressive than usual, trying to prove he was still the same man. She held him tight, letting him know he was everything to her.

August 5, 1988

IT HAD BEEN A LONG TIME coming, but they were finally moving into their very own home. After Dean graduated, he got a job teaching and coaching in a junior high school. They'd moved out of student housing into a bigger apartment.

But the apartment was too small for two active girls. After a year they decided the girls needed a yard to play in, so they bought a house, a fixer-upper. It was a new experience for Claire, but she learned to paint and sew. She made curtains, another first. Dean did all the repairs to the rotted wood and broken gingerbread trim.

They had to completely gut the kitchen and start over.

A friend of Dean's did the cabinetwork and matched it to the dark wood in the house. It turned out beautiful. Claire and Dean would be in debt for the next twenty-five years, but they loved their new home.

The girls ran around giggling, loving the sound of their voices in the big rooms. Sarah said they lived in a castle and that she and Sami were princesses. Claire and Dean had to call them that, too.

Dean said a princess needed a crown, and tried to make one out of construction paper. His efforts were less than stellar, so Claire came to his rescue. Sarah wanted a pink crown and Sami chose purple. To the best of her abilities Claire drew the shapes on paper, and Dean cut them out and taped the ends together. The girls helped with the gluing of glitter and sequins. Soon they had sparkling crowns, which they refused to remove at bedtime.

Claire and Dean tucked them into their new beds, smiling. They tiptoed to the living room and Dean opened a bottle of wine. He filled two glasses and raised his.

"May this house always be filled with laughter."

She touched her glass against his. "And with love."

"Yeah. Lots of love." He took a swallow, then set his wine on the coffee table. "Lots and lots of it." His hand reached for the buttons on her blouse.

"Dean."

"What?" His fingers slid across her collarbone and desire swelled inside her.

"You're not fast enough." She quickly undid the buttons and threw her blouse aside.

He laughed and took off his clothes, and then they were skin on skin as they tumbled onto the area rug. He kissed her until the world spun away and only the two of them remained, wrapped around each other in their own magical castle.

Claire's body welcomed his touch, needed it, and she needed to touch as well, to feel every masculine part of him.

His hardness pressed into her thigh and her fingers trailed down his chest to his stomach. He groaned as she explored and teased secret places only she knew about.

When he could bear no more he rolled onto her, taking her lips as he thrust deep inside her. They fit together perfectly, as they always had. Her hips met each thrust as they rode together to reach the ultimate climax of pure pleasure. His moan of release came a moment after hers.

Afterwards, they lay entwined, their sweat-bathed bodies sated and complete, in a way they knew was as perfect as it could get.

Neither wanted to move or break the physical and spiritual connection they shared. After a few minutes Dean kissed her one more time and rolled away, pulling her up. They sat on the rug drinking wine, kissing and talking. They had truly christened the house as theirs.

And Claire was happy.

November 17, 1988

WHEN IT WAS time for Sarah to start kindergarten, Claire enrolled for morning college classes. Bunny had agreed to watch Sami, and Claire was so excited. Finally, everything was falling into place.

The doctor had been right about Sarah. As she got older, her asthma seemed to disappear. She had flare-ups, but they weren't so frightening. Now Claire could go to school without feeling she was neglecting her children.

She awoke at five to prepare for an eight o'clock class, and to get Sarah ready for school and Sami ready for Bunny's. Dean drove the girls while Claire hurried to class.

That afternoon she picked up Sami and headed for Sarah's school. She stopped for a red light and listened to Sami's chatter. Her daughter held her Cabbage Patch doll, Patty, telling Claire everything she and Bunny had done.

"Grandma put stuff on her hair and it made it really red, Mommy."

"It did?"

Sami nodded. "I want red hair."

Claire suppressed a smile. "Sweetie, you have beautiful blond hair. I would be sad if your hair turned red."

"Oh." She thought about it for a minute. "Patty and me like blond, too."

"Good."

"Sarie does, too."

"Yes. She does." Sami idolized her older sister and followed her around like a shadow.

The light turned green and Claire drove on. She glimpsed something out of the corner of her eye, then heard and felt the crash of metal and glass as a truck slammed into her car, on Sami's side. The force of the impact hurled them into an electrical pole.

Claire lost consciousness for a few seconds, but when she awakened steam was billowing from under the hood. Despite the pain in her head she only had one thought. *Sami!* She had to get to her baby.

Blood trickled down Claire's face and soaked her blouse. Her body ached, but she gathered herself quickly and turned to see how Sami was. Claire's veins turned to ice when she saw how the side door had caved against her child. All she could see was blond hair and blood. Blood was everywhere.

OhmyGod!

She frantically yanked on her door, but it wouldn't open.

"Ma'am." A man came to the broken-out window. "Are you okay?"

She wrestled with the door handle. "Get me out of here, please. I have to get to my daughter."

"Stay calm, ma'am, an ambulance is on the way. Your car is against an electrical pole and you have to be careful."

"Open this damn door, do you hear me?" She heard her voice and realized she was screaming, but she didn't care. All she wanted was to get to her baby.

When the man didn't respond, she undid her seat belt and started to climb through the shattered window.

The man opened the door then and she crawled out. For a split second she swayed dizzily, then groped her way around the car. Traffic had stopped and people had gathered, but she barely noticed. The truck had bounced off her sedan and now blocked two lanes of traffic, with smoke rolling from beneath it.

As she caught a glimpse of her vehicle, her heart stilled and she couldn't breathe. The mangled, crushed door had Sami trapped, and fear like she'd never known before brought Claire to her knees.

She was vaguely aware of the man helping her to her feet, and then she attacked the door, trying with all her strength to drag it off Sami. The wail of sirens didn't stop her efforts.

Two paramedics pulled her away and another held her so she couldn't see what they were doing.

"Call my husband," she sobbed into the man's chest.

She heard the crunch of metal, the buzz of a saw and the shout of a paramedic. "She's alive! Let's get her to the hospital."

Claire sagged limply and the attendant tried to get her into an ambulance. "Please, ma'am. We have to check you over."

"I have to be with my daughter."

"That's not wise. She's—"

Claire tore away and ran to the stretcher where they had laid Sami. Claire took a breath and refused to weaken at the sight. Her daughter was bloody from head to toe. Her little chest seemed caved in and her right leg was twisted.

"Let's go," one paramedic yelled. "We have to keep her breathing."

They loaded the stretcher in an ambulance, and when Claire followed, a man tried to stop her again. "Please, ma'am, you don't need to see this."

She glared at him. "This is my child and she goes nowhere without me." Saying that, she climbed in beside her.

By superhuman control, Claire held herself together. She had to. She reached for Sami's lifeless hand and talked to her. She wanted her baby to hear her voice, so she'd know her mommy was there.

There was a gash in Sami's head, which the paramedics had bandaged, to stop the bleeding. But her precious face was so bloody, her eyebrows were caked with it. Her beautiful blond hair was now blood-red. Claire choked on the horrible quirk of fate. She started to pray, beg and beseech. "Please, don't take my baby."

Within a matter of minutes they were at the hospital, but it seemed like hours. The doors of the ambulance swung open and Sami was rolled away. Suddenly, Dean was there, and Claire fell into his arms. Up until then she'd been able to maintain a measure of composure, but the moment she saw him she burst into tears.

He held her tight. "Honey, don't."

"Sami—" She hiccupped and wiped at her face with the backs of her hands, noticing her tears mingling with the blood. "We have to go…"

They hurried inside as the E.R. team went to work on their little girl. The doctor didn't say much, just that Sami had severe internal injuries requiring immediate surgery. Dean signed the necessary papers.

Another doctor looked at the bruise on Claire's head, but she refused treatment. When Dean insisted, she went through tests she didn't remember afterward. Her only concern was for her daughter.

The doctor said Claire had a concussion, but otherwise was okay. She and Dean sat outside the operating room, waiting and praying.

Then it hit her. "Sarah! I didn't pick up Sarah."

"Don't worry. She's with Mom."

"Oh." Claire sagged against Dean, feeling his strength and his warmth.

"Try to relax, honey," he said. "It's going to be a long wait."

"Dean…"

"Don't say it."

But she couldn't keep the words inside. "Her little chest was crushed and her leg was twisted. What if…?"

"The doctors will fix them," he replied in a hoarse voice, the only sign that he was keeping his emotions in check.

They held on to each other as the wait continued.

"Dean, do you know what happened?"

"The police said a man ran a red light."

"My light was green. I...I—"

"You didn't do anything wrong. Don't even think it."

She drew a sharp breath. "Sami is hurt bad. She could... die." Claire said the one word that neither of them wanted to acknowledge or voice.

Dean jumped up and rammed his hands into his pockets. "Don't say that. I don't want to hear it."

She trembled at the anger in his voice. They were both close to the edge, not knowing if they could survive the next few hours.

They heard the hurried footsteps before they saw her. Bunny rounded the corner at a run, with a carryall in her hand. She ran into Dean's arms and hugged her son. Claire rose from her chair and Bunny grabbed her, the three of them hugging.

"How's Sami?" she asked, her voice shaky.

"She's in surgery," Dean answered. "The doctor said it could be awhile."

"Lord, have mercy." Bunny wiped away a tear. "I called the church, and everyone's praying for Sami and y'all."

"Thanks, Bunny." Claire tucked her hair behind her ears. "Where's Sarah?"

"Your friends, Tim and Nita Mallory, came by and picked her up. They thought I might want to come to the hospital."

"That was nice of them. Sarah loves the Mallorys and playing with Paige."

"They were going to get pizza, and the girls were dancing around. Nita said Sarah could spend the night. I told her I would call later."

Claire chewed on her lip. "Sarah has never been away from us. When it gets dark, she'll want to come home."

Bunny touched Claire's cheek. "Then I'll go get her."

"Did you tell her anything?" Dean asked.

"No. I figured that would be your job."

"Thanks, Mom. We just have to get through this day."

Bunny reached for the bag on the floor. "I brought you some clean clothes, sugar." She handed Claire the bag.

They had cleaned Claire up in the E.R., but her clothes were still covered in dried blood. "Thanks, Bunny. I'll change later."

Suddenly Dean reached for her hand, clutching it tightly. She saw all the worry in his eyes, and was sure it was reflected in her own. But there was nothing they could do but wait.

They turned to resume their seats, and Claire froze.

Her parents stood a few feet away.

CHAPTER FIVE

SHE HADN'T SEEN HER parents in years, and she had nothing to say to them, especially now.

"We heard what happened on the news," her father said, and Claire noticed his hair was turning gray.

"Claire, we're so sorry." Her mother stepped forward and Claire took a step back.

"Why are you here?" she asked numbly.

"Samantha is our granddaughter," Gwen replied.

"That never mattered before." Claire heard the anger in her voice and realized she didn't have the strength to deal with her parents. Not today. She swallowed back the resentment. "She prefers to be called Sami."

Dean squeezed her hand and they turned to see the doctor walking toward them. His face seemed drawn, almost haggard, and Claire knew his news would not be good. She gripped Dean's hand tighter.

Dr. Halsey stopped inches from them. "Sami's in recovery and soon she'll be moved to the pediatric intensive care unit."

"And...?" Dean prompted.

He removed his surgical cap. "Her internal injuries were severe. Her chest cavity was full of blood and her bowels and female organs were severely bruised. We did the best we could, but I'm afraid we had to remove one of her ovaries."

Claire and Dean didn't say anything because they knew the worst was yet to come. "Her chest was basically crushed and her ribs fractured. She was in acute respiratory distress and we now have her on a ventilator."

Dean swallowed hard. "What about her leg?"

The doctor took a breath. "Her right femur is broken, and her kneecap fractured, as is her hip. We've wrapped her femur tightly in position, and a specialist will look at her leg in the morning. Right now our main concern is to keep her breathing."

"What's her prognosis?"

"I'm not going to lie to you. The next twenty-four hours are crucial and…" He stopped talking and twisted his cap.

"And?" Dean asked.

Dr. Halsey looked up. "I've told the nurses in PICU you can stay with your daughter as long as you want. I…I'm sorry…I really don't expect her to make it through the night."

Claire moaned and her knees buckled. Dean caught her and they held on to each other. The world stopped turning. Everything stopped in that moment. This was the one thing they would not be able to survive, and they both knew it.

Claire looked over Dean's shoulder to her mother's worried face. The same face she'd seen when she was nine years old and a car had nipped her bicycle from behind and sent her flying into the street. Her mom had held her, telling her she was fine and everything was going to be okay.

Claire suddenly needed to hear that again.

In a trancelike state she moved from Dean's arms to her mother's. Her mom held her and Claire sobbed as she had when she was nine years old. "Shh, sweetheart," Gwen said. "Everything will be fine." She wiped away Claire's tears. "Go to your daughter."

Claire turned and went back to Dean. His arm went around her waist, holding her up. She was drained and spent, but her daughters needed her.

She looked at Bunny. "Let Sarah spend the night with the Mallorys. If she has an asthma spell or wants to come home—"

"Don't you worry, sugar." Her mother-in-law hugged her. "I'll take care of it. Y'all just look after Sami."

Claire and Dean walked to the elevators. Once inside, she wrapped her arms around his waist and sobbed brokenly. He cried, too. They had come so far and neither was sure how to handle this.

Finally he ran his fingers through her hair and gazed into her face. "Listen, we have to believe in miracles. We have to believe our love will pull Sami through. We have to believe…"

She looked into his watery blue eyes. "I believe."

The doors opened and they walked hand in hand to see their daughter.

Neither was prepared for the sight of their critically injured child. Besides the ventilator, there was a tube in her neck and one in her chest. Her head had been shaved and her beautiful blond hair was gone. Several stitches slanted on the right side. Round disks were attached to her chest and head, with wires connected to a machine. Her small body was swollen to twice its normal size and she didn't look like their little girl.

It took Claire a moment to remember to breathe.

But Sami was alive.

They clung to that.

The night wore on and they sat by her bedside, talking to her, willing her to keep fighting.

"Hey, little princess," Dean said. "We were going to

play ball this afternoon. You can't let me down. Sarah throws like a girl. You said that, remember? Come on, princess, keep fighting. Keep fighting for Daddy. I…"

When Dean's voice cracked, Claire took up the slack. "Mommy's here, baby. I almost have your princess gown finished. Yours is purple and Sarah's is pink. We're going to have a princess party, and I'll tell you a secret. I bought high heels for you and Sarah. Wait till you see them. They have rhinestones, and they're so cool. We will definitely have to call you Princess Samantha. You'll insist on Sami, but Samantha sounds more royal." She paused for a breath. "Baby, Mommy's here."

Toward morning a nurse told them Dean had a phone call. Claire knew it had to be about Sarah. He left, but a minute later was back. Sarah had woken up crying at the Mallorys and wanted to go home. Bunny had picked her up, but Sarah wanted her mommy and daddy.

Claire was torn, but she knew which daughter needed her most. "Go talk to Sarah and I'll stay here," she told Dean.

"No." He shook his head. "I'm not leaving you or Sami. I told Mom to bring Sarah to the hospital, and I'll go down and explain what happened. She needs to know."

"Dean…"

"Honey, we have to take this one step at a time, and we can't leave Sarah in the dark."

Claire nodded, wondering just how much more they could handle.

When Bunny brought Sarah to the hospital, Claire was the one who went out to talk to her. She was Sarah's mother, and felt she had to do it. What with football and coaching, Dean was in and out of their daily lives. Claire was the one who was always there for them.

She stopped short in the waiting room. Her parents were sitting there, in the same clothes they'd had on earlier. They must never have left.

She didn't have time to contemplate that fact as Sarah threw herself into her arms.

"Mommy. Mommy," her daughter cried.

"Hi, precious." Claire sat with Sarah in her lap. Her blond curls bounced around her shoulders and her big blue eyes stared up at Claire.

"Where's Daddy?"

"He's with Sami."

"Oh. Can we go home now?"

"No. Sami's been in an accident."

Sarah twisted her hands together. "Is she hurt?"

"Yes, baby, she's hurt."

"No, Mommy…" At five, Sarah was very intuitive. Her bottom lip trembled and tears filled her eyes.

Claire just held her. For the first time ever, she didn't know how to reassure her child.

"I want to see Sami," Sarah muttered.

Claire stroked her hair. "Not today, baby. But Daddy will come out and say hi."

"Okay." Sarah drew back.

"Mommy and Daddy will stay here, and Bunny will stay with you."

"Oh." Sarah twisted her hands again.

"You and Bunny can play dress-up. You like that."

"Yeah." She thought for a minute. "Can I see Sami tomorrow?"

"Maybe. We'll see."

"'kay."

Claire hugged and kissed her. "I love you."

"I love you, too, Mommy. And Daddy. And Sami. And Grandma."

Claire handed Sarah to Bunny, who nodded toward Claire's parents.

Reluctantly, she walked over to them. "Why are you still here?"

Her mother's eyes were on Sarah. "She looks just like you."

"Yes. She does, except she has Dean's eyes."

"How's Saman—Sami?" her father asked.

"We don't know. We're just counting the hours, trying to get past twenty-four." Claire paused. "Why are you still here?" she asked again.

Gwen shrugged. "I don't know. We found we couldn't leave." She looked at Sarah again. "Do you mind if I speak to her?"

"I'm sorry. I'd rather you didn't right now. She's confused enough."

Gwen nodded. "I understand."

That shook Claire. Her mother never understood anyone's viewpoint but her own.

"Thank you," Claire said, and returned to Sami.

SAMI MADE IT THROUGH the night and the next day. They were elated, but it was still touch and go. The medical staff removed the ventilator to see how Sami would do, if she could breathe on her own. She did so for about five minutes before she went into distress.

They put her back on the breathing machine, but the doctor said she was showing progress. That was all Claire and Dean needed to hear.

It gave them hope.

Claire never left the hospital. Dean came and went, helping with Sarah. The days became long and stressful, but then Sami opened her eyes, a turning point at last.

She made remarkable strides and was soon able to breathe on her own. Her leg became the focus of attention then. They'd waited so long for surgery that the experts suggested Sami be moved to Texas Children's Hospital in Houston, as the operations to her leg and hip would be extensive, and the best specialists were there. Sami, Claire and Dean then took a helicopter Life Flight to Texas Children's for a round of surgeries to repair her leg.

Sami's fractured hip was done first, and held in place with several pins. Next, they concentrated on her leg. The specialist said the Austin doctors had done an excellent job of keeping it straight, something that was crucial for it to grow properly.

Claire and Dean were unprepared for what was to come. After Sami's kneecap was replaced, two metal pins were inserted into the bone on each side of her knee, and weights and pulleys were attached. Sami was in traction on her back, with her thigh perpendicular to her body. Her calf rested in a sling parallel to the bed, keeping her leg in alignment, to heal properly.

After the surgeries, Dean returned home to care for Sarah. It was the first time Claire and he had spent an extended time apart, and it took its toll on Claire's spirit. But she stayed strong for Sami. They spent Thanksgiving and Christmas in the hospital, and tried to make the most of it. Dean and Sarah came on the weekends—and sometimes Bunny did, too. Claire's parents sent gifts and called, but didn't ask to visit, and she was glad they realized she couldn't deal with anything else.

Claire lived for the moment Dean would arrive. Her burden lifted for that brief time and her world righted itself.

When Sami screamed and pleaded for the pain to stop, Claire sometimes neared her breaking point. Having her child in pain was almost her undoing. She would focus on Dean and picture his face, and tell herself that soon he would be there and everything would be okay.

Sami was alive and going to make it.

But there were times Claire wondered if she would.

CLAIRE STRETCHED her shoulders, feeling drained. That time had tested their love, their marriage and their faith. It was still painful to think about.

She went into the kitchen for peanut butter crackers. Munching on one, she unfolded another letter.

My darling Dean,

Today is Valentine's Day and I'm reminded of how much I love you. My parents said we didn't know what love was all about. But they were wrong. We knew even then.

This will be the first Valentine's Day we won't spend together. I miss you and...

Valentine's Day, 1989

"MOMMY, WHY YOU CRYING?" Sami asked, looking so small in the bed, attached to the pulleys.

Claire wiped away tears and smiled at her child. She was so pale and thin, but soon they'd be able to go home.

Claire missed her husband and her oldest daughter and she found that hard to hide.

"I miss Daddy," she said, kissing Sami's cheek.

"I miss Daddy, too." Tears filled her little girl's eyes, and Claire realized she could solve this problem.

She clasped her hands together. "Then let's call him and Sarah."

"Yay! Yay!" Sami shouted. Her voice was weak, and she didn't move a muscle. She had learned that moving caused pain, and she was very protective of her leg.

As Claire picked up the phone, the door opened and Dean walked in, smiling. He was carrying a bouquet of roses and a teddy bear.

She dropped the receiver and ran into his arms. He held her closely, and she needed that.

"What are you doing here?" she finally asked, kissing his lips, his cheek and then his lips again.

"I had to see my girls on Valentine's Day."

"Daddy."

Dean handed Claire the flowers with a long kiss, and then went to Sami, laid the teddy bear beside her and kissed her.

"We miss you," Sami said.

"I miss you, too, baby."

"I want to go home. I want to see Sarie and Grandma."

"Soon, sweetie."

Dean spent the night with them, and it was a Valentine's Day Claire would remember forever.

He was always there when she needed him the most.

AFTER TWO LONG MONTHS, Sami was ready to come home. After she came out of traction, she was put in a body cast that wrapped around her chest and halfway down her good leg all the way down the broken leg. There was a small opening in the crotch so she could go to the bathroom. It would be difficult, but they were going home.

The moment Claire stepped into her house, she felt normal again. They all did. That night she slept in her husband's arms for the first time in months, and gave thanks for all they'd been given back.

BUT THEIR LOVE WAS TESTED to the limit in the months that followed. Sami took up all her time, and Claire forgot about college. They used a wagon to pull Sami around in the house. Sarah loved doing that for her sister.

After six weeks the cast finally came off. Sami's muscles had severely atrophied and she had to undergo extensive therapy. The therapist was trying to teach her to walk again, but Sami only wanted Claire and Dean to carry her.

Claire was never very good at being stern with the girls, but she had to force herself now to be a strict disciplinarian. When Sami cried, Claire made her put weight on her leg, anyway. When Sami screamed at the pain, Claire forced her to take a couple of steps. The strain was once again getting to Claire. Dean tried to help, but Sami wanted only her mother.

Finally, Dean took over caring for Sami on weekends. When Sami cried, wanting Claire, he let her. It wasn't easy for any of them, but they knew they were doing what was best for their daughter. She had to gain confidence and stop being clingy. She had to know they loved her and would always be there for her.

The situation was taking a toll on Sarah, too. She started having frequent asthma spells and throwing tantrums when she couldn't get her way. Claire didn't know how to put her family back together again.

June 23, 1989

SARAH CRIED AND BOUNCED her heels up and down on the hardwood floor because Claire said she couldn't have any more candy. Sami was on the sofa, sobbing. It was time for her to walk and she didn't want to. Dean was teaching summer school because they needed the money, and it was an hour before he was due home from work.

Claire was ready to pull out her hair when the doorbell rang. The last thing she needed was company, but with a sigh, she went to answer it anyway. Her parents stood there. She hadn't seen them since Sami had been admitted to the hospital. They'd called, but the time had never been right for a visit or a talk.

"Oh," Gwen said, hearing the crying inside. "This must be a bad time."

"Yes, I'm afraid it is."

Gwen touched her cheek. "Darling, you look so tired."

The comment didn't sting like it normally would. "I have a lot on my plate at the moment." The crying turned up a notch.

Gwen pushed past Claire and walked into the den. "What's all the fuss about?"

The moment the girls heard a strange voice they stopped crying. Sarah jumped to her feet. "Who are you?"

Without pausing Gwen replied, "I'm your grandmother."

"No, you're not. Bunny's my grandma."

"You have two grandmothers, Sarah," she said.

"Oh." The little girl had nothing else to say. Neither did Claire. Evidently her parents wanted to know their grandchildren. Claire was happy to realize she had no ill feelings about that. But she and Dean would have to talk about it later.

Claire picked up toys, and her father sat in an overstuffed chair. He pulled a silver dollar from his pocket and held it up, looking at Sami.

"You see this, Sami?"

She nodded.

"It belonged to my grandfather. If you'll walk over here to get it, I'll give it to you."

"She doesn't want to walk," Sarah told him.

"That's a pity." Robert reached into his other pocket and pulled out another silver dollar. "But I brought one for you, too. Would you like it?"

"Yes." Sarah walked over and took it. "Wow." She studied the coin. "It's so shiny."

Robert looked at her sister. "Do you want yours?"

Sami nodded.

"Then come and get it."

Sami glanced at Claire. "Mommy will."

"No." Robert shook his head. "This is a special coin. Only Sami can get it."

Her bottom lip trembled and Claire knew the waterworks were about to start again.

"If you cry, you can't have it."

Sami's doe eyes narrowed on her grandfather. Claire knew her daughter had a stubborn streak a mile wide, and she was unsure what Sami would do.

"Just walk to me," Robert coaxed. "It's not far and you can do it."

To Claire's amazement, Sami swung her legs to the

floor and stood. Holding on to the coffee table, she limped to him and snatched the coin out of his hand.

Robert clapped. "I'm so proud of you." He rose to his feet and held out his hand. "Let's walk some more."

Those doe eyes nailed him. "You got more coins?"

He smiled. "A pocketful."

"'kay." Sami took his hand and they walked around the den.

So easy. Why had it been so difficult for her? Claire was exhausted and her patience was nonexistent.

But suddenly she felt better.

Then she saw Dean standing in the kitchen doorway.

He wasn't smiling.

CHAPTER SIX

SARAH SAW HIM, too. "Daddy," she screamed, and leaped into his arms.

Sami tried to follow, but fell, and her cries filled the room. "Daddy, get me. Get me," she wailed.

Dean immediately lifted her into his arms beside Sarah, and the crying stopped.

Dean spoke to her parents and they responded, but the atmosphere was heavy with unspoken tension.

"We better go," Gwen said.

Claire looked at her daughters. "What do you say?"

"Thank you for the coin," Sarah replied politely. "It's pretty."

"Yeah," Sami added, her face buried in Dean's shoulder.

Claire walked her parents to the door.

"We'd love to be able to see the girls, Claire," her mother said.

"I'll speak to Dean, but I'm not promising anything."

"That's all we can ask," Robert said, and they left.

Claire went back into the den. The girls were on the sofa, coloring in Sami's Barbie coloring book. Dean wasn't there. She went into the kitchen and he wasn't there, either. As she entered their bedroom, she saw him sitting on the edge of the bed, his face buried in his hands. Her heart contracted at the sight.

"Dean."

He looked up. "How long have they been coming here?" His voice was filled with anguish and her heart twisted a little more.

"This was the first time. The doorbell rang and there they were. I was surprised to see them."

"Isn't it proper etiquette to call first?"

"I've said no before, and I'm sure they wanted to avoid that."

"So they come without an invitation and my kid walks for him. She won't walk for me but—"

"Dean…"

"When I saw them here I thought you were taking the girls and leaving me."

"What?"

"Life has been so hard. We have bills coming out of our ears, and I'm sure Robert could afford to pay all the medical bills and throw in around-the-clock nurses for Sami. And your life would be much easier."

Claire slid onto his lap and into his arms. "Listen to me, Dean Rennels. I'm taking care of our daughter, not a nurse. And I'm not going anywhere. I love you."

"I don't know why. You should be living in a palace."

She ran her fingers through his hair. "Haven't you heard? We live in a castle and our daughters are princesses!"

"Claire." He rested his face against her neck and she felt him tremble.

"Yes. It's been rough, but our insurance has paid a lot of the bills. We can handle the rest. Our daughter is alive. Now we have to keep pushing her so she'll make a full recovery." Claire kissed his forehead. "She won't walk for you because she knows her daddy will carry her. Her favorite phrase is 'Daddy, get me.'"

"I'm not very strong when it comes to the girls…or you."

"That's called love. Love makes us weak."

He kissed her collarbone. "You make me strong, and it was killing me to think you might be leaving."

"I'm afraid not. You're stuck with me."

He raised his head and kissed her deeply. "I love you," he whispered.

"Mmm." She cradled his head. "Please remember I love you, too, and our love will get us through this rough patch. I believe. Do you?"

He grinned. "Oh, honey, I believe."

"Daddy, look." Sarah came running, showing Dean the coin. "It sparkles."

"Very nice," he said. "We have to put it in a special place so you won't lose it."

"'kay."

"Oh, Mommy, Daddy," Sarah cried excitedly, pointing to the door. Sami was there, holding on to the door frame, her coin clutched in one hand.

"Come on, Sami," Dean coaxed. Claire slipped off his lap and he stood. "Walk to Daddy, baby."

"Get me, Daddy."

Claire saw Dean swallow and knew how hard this was for him. Suddenly he fell to the floor, rubbing his old knee injury. "Daddy's knee hurts. I need a kiss to make it better."

Sarah immediately gave him a big kiss.

"Thank you, sweetie. Daddy needed that, but I need one from Sami, too. Both my girls have to give me a kiss."

Sami stared at her father, and Claire could see all the fear in her beautiful eyes. Claire mentally willed her to walk to Dean, because she knew how much it meant to him.

"Come on, baby, take a step," he pleaded.

"Daddy, get me."

Dean faked a groan and grabbed his knee.

Sami let go of the door frame and waddled to him. "I coming, Daddy. I coming." She fell into his arms and kissed his cheek with a loud smack. "Better?" she asked.

"Oh, a lot better." He held both his daughters and looked at Claire over their blond heads. *I believe,* he mouthed.

That night they made love like they were eighteen, just needing to feel young again and to renew their love.

She lay replete in his arms, not wanting to move. But there was something they had to talk about—her parents. Trailing a finger through his swirls of chest hair, she said, "My parents asked to see the girls."

"What did you say?"

"That I had to talk to you."

He scooted up against the headboard. "So you're thinking about it?"

She scrambled to her knees and pushed her hair away from her face. "I don't feel all that resentment anymore."

"When you and Sami had the accident, you hugged Gwen, and I think your feelings started to change."

"I never realized how much I needed my mother."

"It was their choice, Claire."

"I know." She sank back on her heels. "I often wonder what we'd do if Sarah or Sami fell in love at eighteen and got pregnant with a boy we didn't approve of."

Dean poked a finger into his chest. "The boy you fell in love with was me, Claire, and I was a good kid. I never got into trouble. I made good grades and excelled in sports. It was just their snobbish attitude."

"Yes. A part of me will never forgive them for what they did to us. But there's also a part of me that…" She drew a shaky breath. "I miss my parents, Dean."

"Oh, honey." He pulled her into his arms. "What do you want to do?"

She loved him all the more for his caring, sensitive nature. "Take it slow. Set some ground rules and see how it goes."

"And what would the ground rules be?"

"They can only visit the girls here, and when we say they can. They are not to interfere in our lives or criticize us. They are not to offer us money or buy the girls expensive gifts. And they are to treat my husband with respect."

"Sounds good to me."

"So you're okay with it?"

"Yes. It will take some adjusting, but it's time to be a complete family."

She straddled his hips. "You are so wonderful."

"Mmm." He kissed her long and deep, and she moved her hips against him.

He groaned and muttered, "Before you completely seduce me, what *would* we do if one of our girls got pregnant?"

"We would love her, support her and be there for her because our love is unconditional."

"You got it, lady." He flipped her onto her back, and her giggles filled the room.

CLAIRE HELD ON TO THAT MEMORY a second longer, and then let it go. She moved uncomfortably. How she wished life had been a fairy tale after that, but it had been one crisis after another, with the girls and with her parents. Claire often wondered if their love would survive life's daily struggles.

Her eyelids grew heavy and she drifted into a restless sleep.

THE NEXT MORNING Claire stirred and realized she was still on the sofa, the letters strewn around her. She gathered them up and was stacking them on the coffee table when suddenly, her stomach rolled. She ran for the bathroom.

After rinsing her mouth and washing her face, she headed for the kitchen and coffee. She realized she'd have to cut back on caffeine, and wine, too.

Oh God! She needed caffeine, though—preferably a latte.

As she wrestled with her conscience, the sun peeked over the horizon and bathed the lake with an iridescent glow. She always loved the early mornings and that first sleepy, drowsy glimpse of the world before the busy boldness of the day.

She moved toward the windows to get a closer look, and stopped short. Dean lay in a lounge chair, sound asleep. She stared at his six foot four inches curled up on the too-small lounger, his arms folded across his chest and his dark hair falling across his forehead.

He didn't look much older than the boy she'd married. But he was. They both were. In a moment of clarity she acknowledged that this pregnancy was hard for him, too. He'd always been her number-one supporter, wanting her dream to come true. Ironically, it wasn't his support she needed right now.

Suddenly, unexpected anger shot through her. She'd asked him to leave, but yet there he was, sleeping uncomfortably when he could be home sleeping in their bed.

Because he thought she couldn't handle the pregnancy alone.

When they'd first married, he'd been the one to make all the decisions. She realized that had been because she was so young and inexperienced. But she had left eighteen behind a long time ago. The enormous responsibility of raising two children had catapulted her into adulthood quickly, especially when she was in Houston with Sami. Claire had learned to be independent and strong, and to make decisions for her child, herself and her family. Under dire circumstances, she had developed an inner strength that came with maturity. She'd learned to survive.

And she could handle this pregnancy. She just needed time. That's why she had come to the lake house—to be alone with her thoughts about the past, the present and the future. And she didn't need Dean to hold her hand. Why couldn't he give her the time she wanted?

Marching into the kitchen, she made coffee, but the aromatic scent made her feel sick. She rushed to the bathroom again, to throw up.

I'm too old for this, she kept thinking.

Feeling on the right side of green again, she poured Dean a cup of coffee and carried it to him.

When she opened the door, he stirred and sat up, stretching. "Morning."

She handed him the steaming cup and took the other lounger. "Why didn't you go home?"

"I couldn't." He sipped the strong brew.

"I asked you to."

"I sat in the car for a long time and called our friends. I told Nita and Joan you weren't feeling well, and they both said for you to phone when you're up to it." He cradled the cup, watching her. "You're angry."

"Yes." She pushed back her hair with both hands. "I have to come to terms with this on my own."

He frowned. "I don't understand that."

"I'm sorry."

"We've always made decisions together. I don't understand why this is different."

"No." She shook her head. "That's not true. You made decisions all the time without asking for my input."

His frown deepened. "Like what?"

"You went for that coaching interview in Oklahoma without asking how I felt about it. Nor did you ask how I would feel moving so far away from our daughters."

"Honey, there was no way I was going to get that job. I was even surprised I got an interview. It was all about getting my name out there, so the university athletic directors will know I'm ready to coach on the college level."

She knew that. Why was she being so bitchy? "It's just sometimes I feel like we've lost that special connection."

"What do you mean?"

"I mean you're obsessed with football and I'm obsessed with finishing my education. We used to be obsessed with each other."

"If we were not still obsessed with each other, we wouldn't be in this predicament."

Any other time she would laugh at that statement, but not today. "I'm not thinking straight."

"Honey, just come home."

She looked out at the lake, at the bold morning sunlight caressing its surface. "I thought about the wreck last night and all the pain and heartache we went through."

"But we never gave up, and Sami's a healthy young woman today."

The "we" held Claire riveted. It had been them fighting together to save their child. Dean had worked with Sami on her exercises and stretches to make her leg stronger. Then they'd discovered her leg wasn't growing like the other one, and so began a round of growth hormone drugs.

"Yes. We were lucky," Claire said. "I'm proud of both our girls."

"Me, too. I can't imagine a life without them." He swiped a hand across his unshaved jaw. "Do you regret having them?"

"Not for one minute." She didn't even pause—that motherly feeling inside her was still intact. She'd made the right decision years ago. Now she had to find the courage to make this decision with the same resolve and strength.

He fiddled with his cup, as she'd seen him do a million times. "Do you regret marrying me?"

She looked into those beautiful blue eyes. "You know the answer to that. I've loved you since third grade."

"Claire…"

"What if the baby has Down syndrome? At our age that's a very real possibility." There it was—the fear inside her. The one person she told all her fears to was sitting across from her.

He set his cup on the redwood table. "We'll deal with it like we have everything else."

She closed her eyes and swallowed, needing to say what she had to. "I don't know if I have the strength or capability to go through that."

"Claire, honey…"

"I know it sounds awful."

"It's a very human reaction."

"It's a selfish reaction."

He scooted forward. "Honey, listen. I'll help all I can. The baby won't be due until about March, right?"

"Right."

"Basketball season will be winding down and I'll be able to help out. During the summer I'll take over completely."

"It's not about help, Dean. It's about *me*. I don't want another child." Claire sucked air into her tight lungs as the truth hung between them—her ugly truth.

"I know you, and that feeling will pass," he said. "You'll accept this like all the other things we've had to face. And you are going to college."

She jumped up as anger shot through her once again. "See, you're making decisions again. Go home and give me the time I need to let go of this stupid dream." The words came out louder than she'd wanted, but she couldn't control the anger and resentment inside her.

He rubbed his hands together. "I feel like you're shutting me out." His voice came out low, but she heard it.

She wanted to deny what he'd said, but the words wouldn't come. Maybe this was the one thing they couldn't survive. She'd given up so much and she felt empty inside. She hated herself for that feeling, but couldn't change it.

"This is why I need time alone. I don't want to say things that will hurt you. I just want you to respect my wishes."

He stood. "Okay."

"I'll be home by the end of the week and I'll know what I'm going to do."

"Claire…"

The sound of a car stopped him.

"Are you expecting someone?" he asked.

"No." She glanced at her watch. "It's barely eight o'clock."

Then they heard voices, familiar voices—their daughters.

She turned to Dean. "Did you tell them you were coming here?"

"No."

"How did they find us?"

"I don't know."

"What are we going to tell them?" She wasn't ready to face her daughters.

He looked directly at her. "The truth."

CHAPTER SEVEN

TWO SLIM BLONDES WALKED toward the house, Sami in the lead. Sarah always seemed to be a step behind. Dean thought that odd, since Sami was the one who'd had an aversion to walking for almost two years. Claire had tutored her at home until they decided it was time for her to be with other kids.

That's when Claire had applied for a job as a teacher's aide, so she could be at the school in case Sami needed her. Sending her to school had been the best decision they'd ever made. At first it was rough, as Sami resisted every step of the way, crying and screaming for them.

Once she was in a social environment though, she thrived. She wanted to walk and be like other kids, so she tried harder. At six years of age, she had an exercise program she and Dean did every day. If he was busy with school activities, she was waiting for him when he got home. At times he didn't feel like exercising, but he did it for her.

It paid off big-time. Sami blossomed, and became determined to be a normal child. She turned into an ace tennis player, so good she could have made a career out of it, except that after several rigorous matches her leg inevitably would fail her and she'd fall. So she did the next best thing: she taught tennis, and loved it.

Sami took after Dean in so many ways, but Sarah was a reflection of Claire, except for the blue eyes. Her head was always in a book, and she disliked any kind of exercise, especially anything that messed up her hair.

Sarah was always late, and they argued about that a lot. She had to check her makeup, fix her hair and change her clothes at least three times before leaving the house. But she was driven and determined, and Dean knew she'd inherited those qualities from him.

At almost twenty-five she was finishing a law internship in her grandfather's firm, something Robert had planned for Claire. Sometimes that bothered Dean—maybe because it revealed just how foolish they'd been at eighteen. And it reminded him of everything Claire could have had and could have been—instead of a mother.

And once again he felt he was depriving her of her dream. His chest tightened.

Yesterday their future had looked wonderful. Today…

"Hey, what are you guys doing out here?" Sami hugged her mom and then him.

"How did you find us?" Claire asked, and Dean saw she was nervous, running her hands up and down her arms.

"Sarie and I planned to surprise you this weekend, but you surprised us. You weren't at home."

"So we did the 'what if' theory." Sarah kissed both their cheeks before taking a seat on the lounger and placing the shopping bag she was carrying beside her. "If you're not at home, where would you be?"

"If her theory was wrong, I was planning to strangle her," Sami joked.

Sarah sighed in her true dramatic fashion. "Why we have to be here at this ungodly hour is still beyond me."

"Because we wanted time to visit with Mom and Dad and to give Mom the old rah-rah cheer for college. Then you promised to go with me to a tennis match at one o'clock." Sami winked. "Haven't you heard the early morning does wonders for your complexion?"

"Oh, please." Her sister raised one sandaled foot to look at her painted toenails.

Sami eyed her sister with a gleam in her eyes. "I believe you've put on a pound or two."

"You're not getting me riled with that line, sister dear." Sarah was very diligent about her appearance and constantly watched her weight.

Sami snapped her fingers. "Darn, it usually works."

"We made a deal," Sarah told her. "I'm going to your tennis match and then we're going shopping."

Sami glanced toward the sky. "Just shoot me now."

"Then we're meeting Kip for dinner," Sarah added.

The teasing light in Sami's eyes disappeared. "You're only dating him because Grandpa likes him." She lifted an eyebrow as if daring Sarah to deny it, which took a split second.

"I am not—"

Dean made a time-out sign with his hands before things got heated. "What's this visit about?"

"Oh." Sarah reached for the bag. "We brought Mom a present."

"Yeah." Sami took the bag and handed it to Claire. "We know how excited you are about college, so Sarie and I bought you this backpack. Inside is a digital recorder for lectures so you won't miss a single word. You'll love it."

Claire held the brown-and-green backpack in complete

silence. Suddenly, tears rolled from her eyes, dropping onto the bag.

Dean was immediately on his feet.

"Mom, what's wrong?" Sami put an arm around her.

Sarah reached Claire's side before Dean could. "Mom, what is it?"

"Give your mother some air, girls," he said, and squeezed in to wrap his own arm around her. "She's a little emotional."

"Why?" Sami asked.

He took a deep breath and tightened his arm. Claire seemed frozen. "We just discovered we're having another baby."

There was silence for a whole ten seconds.

"What?" Sami gasped.

Sarah's eyes narrowed. "You're joking, right?"

"No, sweetheart, we wouldn't joke about something like that."

"What are you thinking? You're too old to have a baby." Hurtful words flew out of Sarah's mouth, and Dean didn't like his eldest daughter very much at that moment.

Sami turned on her sister. "Shut up, Sarah."

Claire ran into the house.

There was silence again. No one moved or spoke.

"Sit down," Dean finally said, wanting to go to Claire, but knowing he had to talk to his daughters first.

They sat side by side on the lounger.

"You're so likc Gigi," Sami said to Sarah. "How could you say that to Mom? How could you even think it?"

That was the girls' name for Gwen. Although Robert and she had come into her life late, Sarah was highly influenced by her grandparents. Sometimes Dean regretted allowing his in-laws to get to know his daughters. But Claire needed her parents, and they had worked through a difficult situation together.

"Shut up, Sami. I'm tired of listening to you."

"Don't tell me to shut—"

"Stop it," Dean said in his sternest voice. "I'm very disappointed in you, Sarah. Your mother has always been there for you—always. Right now she needs your love and support, and I expect you to give it wholeheartedly, the same way she has given hers to you. Do you understand me?"

Sarah bit her lip. "Yes, sir. I'm sorry. It just hit me out of the blue. I'm planning to get married and—"

"To that pompous ass?" Sami cried.

Dean held up a hand, stopping them. "I know our lives have revolved around you, but for once this isn't about either of you." He took a patient breath. "Sarah, if you want to get married, you're an adult and free to do so. You mother and I will support you and be there for you. And Sami, please stop the snide remarks. They're not helping."

"I'm sorry," Sami mumbled.

"Sarah, I want you to go inside and apologize to your mother. I'd appreciate it if both of you would offer your love and support. That's what she needs to hear right now."

Sarah ran into the house, and through the window Dean saw them hugging.

Sami got to her feet and watched, too. "Daddy?"

He turned to his youngest child.

"Mom is still going to college, isn't she?"

He shoved his hands into the pockets of his jeans. "We were talking about that when you drove up."

She frowned. "And?"

"We're trying to adjust to this new development in our lives."

"No offense, Dad, but y'all have preached birth control to us since we started our periods. What happened?" She winced. "Forget I asked that. It's probably more information than I really need to know."

"Yes, it is." He nodded. "Just know our love for you will never change."

"Oh, Daddy, please." She threw back her head, her ponytail bouncing. "I'm not jealous of a baby." She swung her thumb toward the windows. "Now the blonde bombshell, that's a whole different set of problems."

"Sarah will come around."

"Yeah, after certain grandparents lavish her with a lot of attention."

Dean noted the resentment on Sami's face. "Why are you so down on your sister?"

"She won't listen to me."

"You mean about Kip Willingham?"

"She's not in love with him." Sami's brown eyes flashed just like Claire's did when she was angry. "But Grandpa and Gigi like him, so she's planning on marrying the guy."

Dean wrapped an arm around Sami's neck and pulled her to him. "Sweetie, you can't choose you sister's boyfriends. Isn't this more about Kip coming between you two? You've always been very close."

"I suppose. We make plans and then she cancels because *he's* made other plans."

"That's called growing up. Soon you'll find someone and have a family of your own, but you and Sarah will always be sisters. So try to get along with Kip. I don't like you being so sarcastic."

"Okay," she muttered, and rested her head on his shoulder. "Daddy?"

"Hmm?"

"Are you and Mom okay?"

"We will be."

He prayed with all his heart that he spoke the truth.

AFTER THE GIRLS LEFT, Claire and Dean walked to the pier and sat with their legs dangling over the side. Not much had changed, but she felt calmer. Touching her girls had reminded her that some sacrifices just couldn't be measured.

Water lapped at the beams of the pier. The roar of a boat could be heard as it neared the entrance of the cove, pulling a skier. It quickly turned and headed for the open lake. The skier waved and water from the wake of the boat sprayed their feet. They waved back.

Then there was just the sound of water lapping.

"You're right," Dean said.

"About what?" She reached down to wipe droplets from her legs.

"You've done all the sacrificing. It's my turn now. I'll stay in the high school coaching job and be there to help with the baby. It shouldn't rest solely on your shoulders."

Claire wanted him to have his dream of coaching college football. He'd put off aggressively pursuing it because of family situations. She wanted her dream, too, but as before, she'd put his needs before her own.

"I wouldn't feel right about leaving my baby." She shook her head. "This isn't really about that. It's how I feel."

"Do you want to talk about it?"

"The thought of 3:00 A.M. feedings, diaper changes,

teething, running after a two-year-old, the constant fatigue and doing the school thing again is giving me chills. I've done my share. I can't…"

He wrapped his arm around her. "It won't be easy."

"People will think we're the grandparents."

"Honey…"

"We shouldn't have to do this again." The anger mounted inside her. "How could we be so stupid?"

"We can't go back. We have to go forward."

"That's what I'm trying to do, but I can't seem to get there."

"I believe we can. Do you?"

She swallowed hard. So many times those words had instilled in her a burning faith that they could overcome anything.

But now…

Dean waited, but she couldn't say it. She felt ashamed, and afraid.

"Remember how frightened you were to drive after the accident?" Dean asked, and for a moment she felt that paralyzing fear. "But you got through it."

She looked at him. "You instilled confidence in me I didn't even know was there."

"Because you knew you had to drive again."

She closed her eyes briefly. "Bunny couldn't keep chauffeuring us around while you were at work. This is different, though."

"Maybe, but…"

"Dean." She scrambled to her feet as everything inside her burst forth. "We wouldn't have to go through this again if you had just had the vasectomy. But it was always after this football season, after this school year, or after our summer vacation. There was always an excuse. You always had an excuse."

His sun-browned skin turned a pasty gray and she felt that shame curl through her once again. She'd never pushed the vasectomy because she knew he had misgivings about it. Somehow her big, strong husband felt it would diminish his sexual drive. And maybe she was a little reticent about that, too. They both enjoyed that part of their life. But right now she didn't want to acknowledge that.

"Saying I'm sorry would be pointless," he stated, his voice hoarse as he stared into the water.

"Yes. And I don't want to talk about this anymore. I came here to be alone so I could come to terms with everything."

With one hand he pushed himself to his feet, his eyes holding hers as the sun highlighted the gray in his hair. "You're so angry."

"Yes, I'm angry. I need to be angry, at myself, at you. So please let me be angry."

"Claire—"

"I'll be home by the end of the week and I'll have made a decision about my future."

He watched her face. "It's not easy to leave you here."

"I want you to."

"Honey…"

"Dean." She sighed in frustration. "This isn't something you can make better, and telling me everything will be fine doesn't help, either."

The worry in his eyes intensified.

They stared at each other for endless seconds. The sun felt warm on her skin, but it didn't reach her heart. Tenderly, Dean kissed her cheek, and the butterfly caress ignited a flame inside her. But she immediately pushed the feeling away.

After a moment he left. She resisted the urge to run after him. When she saw him again, their lives would be different. They would be different.

She wrapped her arms around her waist, and felt a tremor run through her.

Tomorrow would bring changes she wasn't ready to face. She wondered if she ever would be.

CLAIRE WENT BACK TO the house, showered and dressed for the day. The box of groceries she'd brought sat on the counter, and she put them in the cabinet. She'd have to make a trip to the convenience store down the road for milk. She needed to start drinking milk again.

Her hands stilled as that thought ran though her. She was already accepting the pregnancy. It was a start. But she knew she had a long way to go.

Picking up the letters, she tied the red ribbon around them. Memories—wonderful memories. They'd even made the bad times wonderful because their love had been unshakeable.

She clipped her hair back to keep it off her face. All the while she wished she had a stack of letters to tell her their future.

DEAN THREW HIS KEYS on the table and glanced around the quiet house. It wasn't the same without Claire. She filled his home, his life and his heart.

He sat down and stared at the blue-and-yellow flowered curtains she had made for the breakfast room. When they'd first married, Claire didn't know how to cook or sew. But she'd learned.

The cooking was pretty bad at first, but he'd have eaten

sawdust if she'd served it. He taught her what he knew, and Bunny had shown her the rest. Claire caught on easily. She wanted to do everything to please him. Pleasing him was easy; she just had to be in his life.

So many times she'd tried to go back to college. Once Sami was on her feet again and going to school, Claire had enrolled in night classes and Dean kept the girls. But Sami wasn't ready to have her mother not there to put her to bed. Their daughter cried every night, wanting her mommy. He cajoled her and stayed in her room until she fell asleep.

One night class was canceled because the professor was sick. Claire came home to find Sami crying for her. After she got Sami down for the night, she stared at Dean and her eyes were angry.

"Why didn't you tell me she was so upset?"

"Because I knew you'd stop going to class, and I want you to go. Sami is fine. We've just spoiled her."

Claire ran her hands up her arms. "I can't go to class and know my child is in tears."

"Honey." He took her hand and led her to their bedroom. "I have it under control, trust me." He kissed her lips.

"Dean," she moaned, in that way that sent his senses spinning.

"You're not dropping out of class," he told her, pulling her top over her head.

But at the end of the semester, Claire did just that. Her children needed her, and he knew she wasn't happy being away from them.

He wasn't happy without her, either, so another attempt at college had failed....

Jumping up now, he headed for the bedroom, showered

and changed. He and his friends, Tim and Eric, had planned to play golf today while their wives had a day out. He was glad he'd called and canceled. He wasn't in a mood to do anything.

He could hear Claire's words drumming through his head. *If you'd had the vasectomy…*

Oh God. He sank into a chair with a deep sigh. She was right. This was his fault. He'd kept putting it off because he wasn't sure about the procedure and the aftereffects. He had a friend who went through it, and a year later Ron and his wife were divorced.

Ron said the vasectomy had changed him. He didn't have that sexual urgency anymore. Ron tended to be a hypochondriac, and Dean hadn't really believed him. All he'd read disputed that, but the doubt still lingered.

How could he be so macho and stupid? He should have been thinking about Claire instead of his male ego. Now he wondered if she would ever be able to forgive him.

Or if he could forgive himself.

CHAPTER EIGHT

NOT ABLE TO STAY in the house with himself and his thoughts, Dean drove to his mom's. He wanted to see how she was settling in, and he had to tell her about the baby.

He rang her doorbell even though he had a key. He didn't want to startle her.

"Hey, champ," she said, opening the door.

Bunny was now in her sixties, but looked much the same as she had when he was a kid—tall and thin, with her hair still red. She made sure it stayed that way. These days she wore it shorter, though.

She looked behind him. "Where's Claire?"

His mom and his wife were very close. In the years Gwen hadn't been there, Bunny had become Claire's mother.

"I could use a cup of coffee," he said, evading the question.

"You got it."

They walked into her small kitchen. Ads from a Sunday paper were strewn on the table. A pair of scissors lay on top. Bunny was cutting out coupons to use at the grocery store, something she'd taught Claire.

He eyed the boxes stacked in the utility room. "How's the unpacking coming?"

"Fine as frog hair." She placed a cup in front of him and

took her seat, resuming her cutting. "With the move, I didn't get a chance to cut out last week's coupons."

He took a sip of coffee. "I'll help with the unpacking."

"Oh, no." Bunny shook her head. "You've done enough, and I want to be able to find things."

"You could point and tell me where you want stuff."

"Are we gonna chitchat or are you going to tell me why Claire's not with you?" She stopped cutting and glanced at him. "Is she still sick?" Without giving him time to answer, she went on. "Well, for crying out loud. Why didn't you say so?" She pushed back her chair. "I'll make her some chicken soup."

Dean caught her arm. "Mom, I have something to tell you."

"Holy crap." Bunny plopped into her chair. "It's bad, isn't it? I can tell by the look on your face."

He swallowed hard. "Claire's pregnant."

"What?"

"Claire's pregnant. That's why she's been throwing up."

"No." Bunny shook her head. "That can't be. Not now and not after everything she's given up for this family."

"It's true."

"Oh, my, my. You two are like rabbits. You just can't stay away from each other."

"Claire's at the lake house and she's having a hard time with this." He ran his hands over his face. "I'm scared, Mom. This is all my fault."

"Maybe not *all* your fault."

He lowered his hands. "It is. We talked about a vasectomy, but I never had it done. I'm calling for an appointment on Monday." He'd made up his mind.

"Well, now that's kind of like shutting the gate of the

corral after the pony's been out frolicking in the pasture for a while."

"Mom!" She still had the power to shock him. But that was his mother, very blunt.

"Don't give me that look." She pointed the scissors at him. "Before you do anything, you talk to Claire first."

"Yeah." He twisted his cup in his hands. Having it done now wasn't going to solve anything. He and Claire had to talk.

"She just needs time," his mom murmured.

"I don't know. She's not accepting the pregnancy."

"Well, who would at her age? She's raised her kids and did a mighty fine job, if you ask me. She's looking forward to some time for herself and she deserves it." Bunny smacked his arm.

He drew back. "What's that for?"

"For being a man."

For the first time in hours he felt like laughing.

She shook a finger in his face. "You make this right."

"How? When we were eighteen, the answer was easy. We got married and planned to live happily ever after. We both wanted that."

"But this baby takes the happily ever after out of the equation?"

"Pretty much. Claire feels cheated, and I'm not sure we can find a solution this time. That's what scares me."

"Make her feel young and in love again. Everything else will fall into place."

"How do I do that?"

"Oh, champ, if you have to ask your momma that then you're in bigger trouble than I thought."

Dean smiled and leaned over and kissed her cheek.

"Thanks, Mom. You always know what to say." He stood. "I'll talk to you later."

"I'm available for babysitting duties," she shouted after him, then in a lower voice added, "With your track record I'll still be babysitting with one foot in the grave and the other foot on a banana peel. You're sure gonna keep your momma young."

Dean hurried home, going over and over what his mom had said. *Make her feel young and in love again.*

Suddenly he knew exactly how to do that.

CLAIRE OPENED A CAN of soup and made a grilled cheese sandwich. She wasn't hungry, but she ate them anyway. By afternoon the sky grew cloudy and looked like rain. Since the heat wasn't so oppressive, she went outside. As she walked to the pier, she saw Harold Weatherby, their neighbor, walking along the shoreline carrying his dog, Ozzy.

Mr. Weatherby had lost his wife of sixty years three months ago. He seemed so lonely without her.

Claire waved and walked toward him. He met her halfway. The houses in the cove weren't close together and each had privacy. It had been one of the big selling points for her and Dean.

The first thing she noticed as she reached him was Ozzy. He was soaking wet.

"How are you, Claire?" Mr. Weatherby asked, his aged face a mask of sadness.

"I'm good. How about you?"

"I'm very upset with Ozzy."

She stroked the medium size brown-and-white terrier. "What did he do? Take a swim?"

"You could say that. I let him out to play and the next

thing I knew he was across the cove at the Hilmans'." He leaned over and whispered. "He misses Mary Ruth. He keeps looking for her."

"Oh, poor Ozzy. That's why he's wet."

"Yes. Helen called and said Ozzy was barking at her back door. Helen and Mary Ruth visited a lot. She asked if I would please come and get him. I went outside and called several times and he finally swam back." Mr. Weatherby scratched Ozzy behind his ears. Claire knew how much he loved the dog, and Ozzy was all he had left. "You and Dean taking a quiet weekend before school starts?"

Her stomach clenched. "I'm here by myself."

Mr. Weatherby glanced up. "Really? That's unusual. You two are always together. Mary Ruth and I talked about that. You reminded us of ourselves when we were younger."

Mary Ruth and Harold were devoted to each other. Their love was timeless, just as she had often thought hers and Dean's was. The Weatherbys were both professors at the University of Texas and had no children. She wondered how a child would have affected their love.

"Thank you," she said. "That's a very nice compliment." She licked her lips, knowing she was being intrusive, but somehow she needed to know. "May I be so rude as to ask why you never had children?"

"My dear, of course you may ask. Mary Ruth and I met in college and quickly married. When we were stable financially, we tried to have a family, but it never happened. We both went for testing and it turned out that I have a low sperm count." He stroked Ozzy, and Claire knew he was seeing his wife's face. "I thought about it for a long time and I left Mary Ruth."

"You did?" Claire couldn't hide her shock.

"We were separated for two years. I tried to divorce her and she refused. I was very determined she was to have this life I had pictured in my head. A life with children."

"What happened?"

"I was miserable. She was miserable. We decided to be miserable together, but instead we were suddenly very happy."

"That's a wonderful story."

"We thought about adopting, but we were both busy with our careers. The time just never seemed right." His mouth twitched into a semblance of a smile. "To be honest, we were happier with just the two of us."

"It showed," Claire told him.

"There were times when we watched your girls on the lake, swimming and skiing with their friends, and we wondered what it would have been like to have a child. But we believe we were happier alone." He glanced toward the sky. "But without Mary Ruth I am truly alone. I have friends, but it's a loneliness that's hard to describe."

"You have Ozzy," she reminded him, trying to cheer him. The terrier had been a member of the Weatherby household since Claire had known them, about eight years.

"Yes." He cuddled the dog, his cloudy eyes on Claire. "You seem a little down. Are you nervous about college?"

"I…" She wasn't sure what she was going to say, if anything.

"What's that?" Harold frowned toward the bend in the cove near the Hilman house. A plastic cork floated on the water, clearly anchored to something. "Is that a cork?"

"It looks like it."

This was the first time she'd noticed the object, and she wondered how Mr. Weatherby could see it when a month ago he could barely spot a boat on the water. Of course, the cork seemed to be one of the newer ones that reflected the light and sparkled in the water. And the lake was calm today, with no choppy waves for it to hide in.

"I had my cataracts removed three weeks ago and I'm amazed at how much better I can see."

"Oh." That explained it.

"It has to be attached to a fishing line, and someone should remove it. It could be dangerous for swimmers and skiers." He turned in the direction of his house. "Pardon me, Claire, but I must call the lake personnel."

She waved goodbye, walked to their pier and sat cross-legged, watching the plastic object bob up and down. She was sure it was attached to a rod and reel that evidently was hung on something in the water. A big fish must have jerked it out of someone's hand and the current had brought it to the cove. She hadn't noticed it yesterday, so it must have washed in during the night.

Mr. Weatherby was now sitting on his screened-in deck, holding Ozzy and also watching the cork. Soon the lake authorities would remove it. They were very good about things like that.

She thought about her neighbor and his loneliness, and how Ozzy was such good company for him.

May 6, 1992

SARAH'S ASTHMA and allergies prevented them from having a dog, but as she grew older her symptoms lessened dramatically. The doctor cut back on her medication and she rarely needed a breathing treatment.

The girls were eight and nine when a mixed yellow Lab

wandered into their yard. Sami was walking really well by then and she was enthralled with the dog, as was Sarah.

Claire called around to see if any of the neighbors were missing a pet. No one knew where the Lab had come from. She tried to explain very patiently to her daughters that they couldn't keep the dog; it would make Sarah sick.

Two sad faces looked back at her.

"But, Mommy, he doesn't have a home," Sarah said.

Claire tried to keep her away from the dog, with no success. So she brought out the line that always got their attention. "We'll wait until your father gets home."

"That's good, Sarie," Sami whispered. "Daddy likes dogs."

Claire called Dean to alert him.

"How's Sarah?" he asked.

"She seems fine. She's all over the dog, and I can't keep her away from him unless I lock her in the closet or something."

"Hang on. I'll be home in a little bit."

Both girls barreled toward him before he could even get out of the car. "Daddy, Daddy, look," Sarah cried, pointing to the Lab. "God sent us a gift—a very special gift."

"I see," he replied, and glanced at Claire.

She lifted an eyebrow, relieved he was going to handle the situation.

"Daddy." Sami stroked the dog. "He's so beau-ti-ful."

Dean squatted down. "We have to talk, girls."

At that moment the dog licked him in the face, and by his expression, Claire knew they were in trouble. He cleared his throat, running his hand along the animal's back. "I'm sure he belongs to someone, and we have to find the owner."

"Oh." Sami stuck out her lip.

"Can we keep him until then?" Sarah asked.

"Sweetheart, there's a reason we don't have a dog."

She hung her head. "I know. It's me. We can't have anything because of me."

Sami put an arm around her sister. "It's okay, Sarie."

Dean glanced at Claire and she could read his mind. *Let's give it a try.* She nodded, and he pulled Sarah and Sami to him. "Here's the deal, kiddos. Get your poster boards and we'll make signs and put them up in the neighborhood. If no one claims him in a week and Sarah has no reaction, then we'll keep him."

"Oh, boy. Thank you, Daddy." Sarah's eyes lit up. "I won't hardly breathe."

Both girls gave Dean kisses and then joined hands, jumping around. Suddenly they stopped and whispered to each other.

"We named him Barney," Sarah announced.

"Girls..." They knew that tone of voice of their dad's.

"Okay." Sarah nodded. "We'll call him Dog until nobody claims him."

Claire and Dean exchanged another glance, but it was hard to put a damper on their daughters' excitement.

When the two of them ran to get sign-making supplies, Claire said, "I hope we're doing the right thing."

He gave her a lingering kiss. "It's going to be a long week and we have to watch Sarah closely."

Claire poked him in the ribs. "You're such a pushover."

"When it comes to my gals, you bet I am." She met his lips eagerly and got lost in the moment until they heard a loud bark. They drew apart and Dean shook a finger at the dog. "That's not a good start."

Claire wrote on the boards and Dean and the girls

posted them around the neighborhood. The week wore on and Sarah didn't have any breathing problems. Dog slept on the patio in a bed the girls made. Claire checked with the doctor and he said he didn't see a problem, as long as Sarah was watched closely the first few weeks.

One night as they were eating dinner, the doorbell rang. Dean was cutting Sami's chicken, so Claire went to answer it. A woman in her fifties stood there, holding one of the signs they'd made.

Claire's heart sank. She'd grown fond of Dog and she worried about the girls.

"Hi," the woman said. "I'm Tina Carter. My mother lives two streets over and I believe—" she held up the sign "—this is her dog."

"Come in, please." Claire opened the door and called Dean.

He strolled into the entryway followed by the girls. Claire made the introductions, her eyes on Dean.

What are we going to do?

"Dog belongs to you?" Sarah asked, and clung to her dad.

"You can't have him," her sister said, her eyes dark.

Dean lifted Sami into his arms. "Sweetie, remember we made a deal."

"I don't care. She can't have him."

"Sami."

She bit her lip and buried her face in Dean's neck.

"I'm sorry," he stated. "My daughters have grown attached to the dog."

"Oh, don't apologize," the woman said with a wave of her hand. "I've just moved my mother into a nursing home. I've had so much going on I forgot about her dog. When I went to feed him, I realized he was gone, and then I saw the sign."

"What do you plan to do with him?" Dean asked.

"I don't live here so I guess I'll take him to the pound."

"What's a pound?" Sarah asked.

"It's a doggy home," Claire replied.

Sarah frowned. "Dog doesn't need a home. He has a home."

"What my daughter is trying to say is that we would like to keep him."

"Sure, no problem," Mrs. Carter said. "My mother will be happy to know he has a good home."

"Thank you," Claire said, feeling relieved. "We should pay you something."

"Please. It's a load off my mind! He's had all his shots and he's been neutered, by the way."

"That's very generous," Dean added. "And we appreciate it."

"What's his name?" Sarah asked.

Mrs. Carter shrugged. "I have no idea. My brother bought him as a puppy about two years ago, and I believe he called him Sport or something. I really can't remember. I live in Seattle and don't visit that often. My brother got married and his new wife didn't like dogs, so my mother was stuck with him, but he was company for her, I suppose. I could ask my brother if you like."

"No. That's okay," Dean said.

"You don't know his name?" Sarah couldn't get past that.

Sami raised her head from Dean's shoulder. "His name is Barney."

CLAIRE REALIZED THE SUN was sinking, and she'd been sitting on the pier reliving happy memories. She wrapped her arms around her waist. Barney had become a part of their household, and there were times she cursed him and other times she loved him.

When he chewed up the garden hose and the wheels on their lawnmower, she'd wanted to kill him. They learned early, though, that he was a wonderful guard dog.

One day the girls were playing in the front yard, something they didn't normally do, when she heard Barney barking aggressively.

She'd just checked on them and couldn't imagine what had happened in that short amount of time. She hurried to the door and saw that Barney had a man pinned against his car. The girls ran to Claire and she shouted for Barney to get down. She had to shout three times.

There was something about the man that made her skin crawl. She asked what he wanted, and he said he was selling magazines. She asked him to leave, which he did. But she still had a bad feeling.

She called Dean and he informed the police. The man turned out to have a record, and he wasn't selling magazines. It had been a scary episode, and Claire hugged Barney until her arms ached. The girls never played in the front yard again, and when they were outside the dog was with them at all times.

Claire rose to her feet now and slowly made her way to the house. Barney had died the year Sami went to college. They'd lost a true friend. They'd buried him in the backyard, and no matter how busy the girls were when they were home, they always found time to put a dog biscuit on his grave.

Claire opened the door and went inside, breathing in the cooler air. Memories jockeyed for position in her mind, as if each needed to be remembered and treasured.

But she was so tired.

CHAPTER NINE

CLAIRE FELL ASLEEP ON the sofa for a while and then woke up feeling lonely. She was used to having Dean's arms around her and she missed him. She took the clip from her hair and shook it out. Without him everything seemed so quiet. Was that how Mr. Weatherby felt?

Darkness surrounded the cabin, enclosing her in her own private world.

Her own private thoughts.

Even though they'd had hard times, their life had been filled with love. The girls' school years had been so busy that Claire seemed to spend all her time in the car, chauffeuring them to school events, piano and ballet lessons. She didn't even think about college, because she knew she couldn't fit it in. Her daughters still needed her.

Sami had to have the pins removed from her hip when she was twelve, because her body had grown and they were loose. The doctors arranged to have it done during the summer so she wouldn't miss any school. Sami rebounded quickly and astounded everyone with her progress, especially in tennis.

Those years were busy, but happy. Claire and Dean encouraged the girls to be active in school and in sports.

Then the dating started, and she and Dean began to

argue. He was overprotective, but didn't see it that way. The biggest fight they ever had was over one of Sarah's dates. Camden Sayers was a kid who was always in trouble, but for some reason Sarah liked him. She helped him in English and he asked her to a dance.

Dating, 1996

"SHE'S NOT GOING," Dean said stubbornly, that strong chin at an angle she knew well.

"Sarah's thirteen and she's meeting him at the dance. It's not like he's going to pick her up and drive her somewhere. And we're chaperoning the event. I don't see a problem."

"The problem is he's not suitable for my daughter."

"Well, you weren't suitable for my father, so I snuck around to be with you. I don't want Sarah doing that."

He paled visibly. "You know I've spent half my life trying to prove myself to your father, and I'm getting tired of it. I just never realized I had to prove myself to you, too."

"Dean, I didn't mean it that way."

"Sure you did. I've never been good enough for you or your family."

"This isn't about us."

"It is. It's always about us and the bad choice you made in choosing a man."

"Dean…" Claire moved nearer to him, not liking how the conversation was going.

He backed away. "I wasn't some street kid selling drugs or getting into fights. I had dreams and goals and—"

"I know. That's why I love you."

He drew a deep breath. "I work in the school system and

I know this kid. He's into fights all the time and spends most of his time in detention."

"But Sarah sees something in him. Let her find out the rest herself."

"Why? I see no reason to put my daughter through that."

"If we say no, she'll want to go out with him all the more."

Dean's eyes narrowed. "Is that why you wanted to go out with me? Because your parents forbade it?"

"Honey—"

Before she could finish the sentence, he grabbed his jacket and headed for the door. "She's not going out with him and that's my last word." The door slammed shut behind him. In a moment she heard his car rev up and roar out of the driveway.

Tears stung her eyes. Dean had never left before. For a moment she stood there in shock, not knowing what to do.

"Mom." Sarah stood in the doorway, her blond hair disheveled around her face.

Claire quickly got herself under control. "What is it, sweetie?"

"Did Daddy leave?"

She swallowed. "Yes."

"Why? It's late."

"Sarah, go to bed. We'll talk in the morning."

"You and Daddy were supposed to talk about Cam and if I could meet him at the dance. I heard loud voices. Were you arguing?"

Claire bit her lip, not wanting to lie. "Yes. We had a disagreement."

"And Daddy left?" Claire could hear the panic in her voice.

"Yes."

"I don't have to meet Cam, really. The kids treat him like dirt and I didn't want to hurt his feelings. He's not as bad as everyone says he is. I'll just tell him I'm not going." Sarah's voice wobbled. "Is Daddy coming back?"

"Why is everyone up?" Sami stumbled in, rubbing her eyes. Barney was at her feet.

"Daddy left," Sarah told her.

"Go to bed, girls. You have school tomorrow." Claire was trying to keep this from escalating into something it wasn't.

"What do you mean, Daddy left?" Sami was wide awake now.

"He and Mom had an argument over me meeting Cam at the dance, and Daddy left."

Sami made a face and kicked her sister's shin. Sarah screamed and hopped around on one foot. Barney barked, jumping up and down.

"Everyone, stop it this instant," Claire shouted. "And Sami, don't you ever do that again. Tell your sister you're sorry."

"I'm sorry," she muttered, then asked in a low voice, "Why does she have to like boys, anyway?"

The room became quiet. Barney lay down, his face on his paws.

"Go to bed," Claire said in a tired voice. "Your father will be home later."

"I'm sleeping in the den until Daddy comes back," Sami announced, and ran in that direction.

Sarah followed and Claire trudged behind them. The three of them curled up together, waiting. Faithful Barney lay on the area rug, watching them.

The girls drifted off to sleep, but Claire kept looking at her watch. Dean had never been this angry or upset. She'd handled it badly and she didn't know when he was returning. But she knew one thing—he would come home.

Two hours later she heard his key in the lock. She tried to get up, but Sami's leg rested across her lap and Sarah's arm was flung over Claire's chest.

Dean came to an abrupt stop when he saw them. The room was in darkness except for the moonlight spilling in from the windows. Barney rose to his feet and sniffed Dean's shoes.

Dean and Claire stared at each other, but neither said a word.

She shook their daughters. "Daddy's home."

Sami awoke first and hurled herself at him. "Daddy, don't leave us again."

Sarah pushed her hair from her face and ran to Dean, hugging him. "I don't have to meet Cam at the dance. It's not worth you and Mom arguing."

"Hey, what's up with you two? I'm always going to be here," Dean said.

"Promise, Daddy?" Sami asked.

He looked at Claire. "I promise. Now go to bed."

The girls disappeared down the hall, Barney loping behind them.

Claire got up and marched into their bedroom. She pulled the covers back, not saying a word.

Dean removed his jacket and flung it over a chair.

Claire fluffed her pillow with more force than necessary and then turned to face him. "Let's get something straight, Dean Rennels. I love you. I'm always going to love you. It has nothing to do with my parents. It's the way I've felt since I was eight years old. If you don't understand that, then our marriage is in trouble."

He jammed a hand through his hair. "I'm sorry. I over-reacted. I guess that feeling of not being good enough is always going to dog me."

"You're good enough for me. That's what matters. Don't you know that by now?"

He grinned. "Care to refresh my memory?"

She walked to him and slipped her arms around his neck, pulling his head down to hers. Their lips met in an explosion of all the emotions they were feeling.

Claire groaned and wrapped her legs around his waist in an acrobatic movement she didn't even know she could do. They tumbled on to the bed. She kept her legs tight around him and the kiss went on and on. As Dean's mouth trailed to her neck, her maternal antenna went up.

"The girls are at the door," she whispered.

"Go to bed," Dean shouted, and they heard running feet on the hardwood floor.

Claire rolled to one side. "They're just worried. They're not used to us arguing."

He got to his feet and closed the door. Unfastening the buttons on his shirt, he said, "Let's don't do that again."

She pulled her T-shirt over her head and they quickly un-dressed. Dean fell down beside her, gathering her into his arms while she reveled in the sensation of her skin brushing against the rougher male texture of his. They forgot every-thing but the moment and how they made each other feel.

He stroked her body until they both were on fire, and she pulled him between her legs, needing him now. Feeling his strength inside her, she held on to his shoulders, basking in the sheer pleasure only he could give her.

Later, their sweat-soaked bodies lay entwined. He kissed the tip of her nose. "I love you."

She threaded her fingers through his damp hair. "You're everything to me. Everything."

He rolled to her side and pulled her against him. They snuggled, sated and at peace.

"Why were y'all waiting up?" he asked, stroking her arm.

"They heard you leave and were afraid you weren't coming back."

"Why?"

"So many of their friends' parents are divorced or getting divorces, I guess that was at the back of their minds."

"Never." His arms tightened around her. "I'm in this forever."

"So am I." She sat up. "We still have to decide about the dance."

He reached for her hand and interlocked his fingers with hers. "She can go."

"Sarah said she feels sorry for Cam, and he's not as bad as everyone thinks he is. She sees something in him no one else does, and I think he deserves a chance."

"What kind of chance?"

With her other hand Claire poked his chest. "You. You're the junior high coach. Get him into sports. What is it you say?" She thought for a minute and lowered her voice, mimicking his. "Let's see what you're made of, boy."

"Claire…"

"You help kids all the time. You've told me how sports can turn a boy around. Cam is no different, and this is a chance to be a hero in your daughter's eyes."

"Hey." Dean grinned. "I'm already a hero in both my daughters' eyes."

"Yes, you are." Claire stretched out on top of him. "And you've always been *my* hero." She kissed his chest. "So what do you say, Coach? What can you do with Camden Sayers?"

"I'm not sure." He held her head with both hands and captured her lips for a tantalizing moment. "But I know what I can do with you."

"Ah, we both know that." She moaned as his fingers tiptoed down her back. "You can make me dizzier than two glasses of wine. But you're much, much more potent."

Their sighs and laughter mingled with each breath, and the turmoil of the evening was quickly forgotten.

In the morning everyone was in a rush. The girls wolfed down cereal and fruit while Dean had toast and eggs. After, he carried his plate to the sink and refilled his coffee cup, then smiled at Claire over the rim. "We need to argue more often. Makeup sex is oh so good."

"Shh," she whispered as she passed him.

He grabbed her around the waist and kissed her hard.

"Woo-hoo," Sami shouted. "Mom and Dad are back to normal."

Barney barked and Sami gave him some of her dry cereal.

Dean smiled into Claire's eyes and then walked to the table. "Sarah, we've decided you can meet Cam at the dance."

She glanced up from a book she was reading. "Oh, cool."

"But I will be having a talk with Cam today."

Her eyes went wide. "No, Daddy. Please."

"Why?"

"He's scared to death of you. All the boys are."

"What? That's the first I've heard of this."

"You're 'Tougher Than Nails' Rennels. A kid has to produce results or he's gone. Kaput. Out of the program."

"I think you're exaggerating."

"I am not," Sarah retorted. "You know you're tough."

"Well then, let's see what Camden Sayers is made of."

"Oh God." Sarah buried her face in her hands. "I'm never dating again."

"Sounds good to me." Sami stuffed a strawberry into her mouth. "Maybe I'll be able to get in our bathroom every now and then."

Sarah stuck out her tongue at her.

"Sarah," Dean interjected in his fatherly voice. "All I'm saying is Cam might be interested in sports. You told your mother the kids treat him badly. I assume that's why he's always in fights. I'm just going to offer him a way to work off some of that aggression."

"My life is over," Sarah muttered.

Claire intervened. "Your father is doing a nice thing here. Give him some credit."

"But why can't he pick on someone else?" she wailed.

"Get your books." Dean had had enough, and the girls knew that tone of voice. Claire did, too. "I'm leaving in five minutes, unless you want to ride with your mother."

Sami scrambled out of her chair. "I'm going with you, Dad."

"I'm going with Mom." Sarah dragged her feet, as if she were heading to the gallows instead of the den to get her books.

Dean kissed Claire. "Tonight I'll show you just how tough I am. That is, if I don't strangle a daughter first."

When Claire picked up Sarah from school, she was still in a mood. But it was ballet afternoon, and once class started Sarah was back to herself. She was an accomplished dancer and Claire loved to watch her. Claire had never been that graceful and knew her daughter had inherited some of Dean's athleticism.

After the dance that weekend, Camden Sayers became a popular name at the Rennels dinner table. He not only started to play football, he got into baseball and track. Dean talked often about Cam's talent; once the boy applied himself there was no turning back. Because of Dean, he soon had goals and dreams.

He and Sarah never became more than friends. She often joked that her daddy had stolen her boyfriend.

CLAIRE GOT UP and went in search of food. She made a ham sandwich and wished she'd thought to buy milk today. It would be the first thing on her to-do list in the morning.

The house was so quiet with no TV, no voices. She'd often heard the saying that silence was deafening. She now knew what that meant.

Staring at the phone, she wanted to call Dean, to hear his voice. She felt bad about the things she'd said to him. But as she'd told him, she was in anger mode and had to sort through that.

Alone.

She had to figure out why she felt this way.

For twenty-five years she'd dreamed of going to college. That was a long time. Why hadn't she? In the early years Sami's health and well-being had been her top priority. Claire went to work in the school system and found something she loved—teaching. And the dream became more urgent.

But she'd accomplished very little toward her goal of getting her degree. She'd told herself her family came first. But was something else involved here?

When they were offered the deal on the lake house, she was the one who had encouraged Dean to buy it, realizing her dream would be put on the back burner again. A pool and a tennis court were within walking distance, and she rationalized how good that would be for the girls, especially for Sami, who needed daily exercise. Both her daughters would benefit from being outdoors, away from the TV and the computer, not to mention movie theaters on weekends.

Was it more? Maybe subconsciously Claire felt she'd made a mistake by getting pregnant the first time, and was trying to atone by sacrificing her own goals. Could she feel she didn't deserve to have her dream come true? Was that why she didn't fight for it? Why she'd immersed herself so completely in her girls' lives? Why she'd never pushed Dean for the vasectomy? If she had, he would have had it done.

All this musing only angered her more, and she had no answers. Claire realized that first she had to accept the pregnancy. After that, she wasn't sure about her life. Maybe the dream was just that—a dream.

And it was time to let it go.

CHAPTER TEN

DEAN SAT ON THE SIDE of the bed, staring at the phone and fighting the urge to call Claire. He needed to know she was okay. But he'd promised to give her time. He'd never realized how hard that would be.

Getting up, he started to pace, something he did methodically on the sidelines at the football field. It brought the game into focus, and he could sort through plays, signals and strategy. But this wasn't a game.

It was their life.

Their future.

He knew Claire was reliving all the heartache and pain of the last twenty-five years. And he hoped she remembered the joy and the love that had made everything worthwhile. How could she not? It defined exactly who they were—two people deeply in love.

He stopped in front of a bookcase cluttered with family pictures. There was a tiny photo of a young man in uniform tucked into the side of a frame. Camden Sayers.

Claire had been right about Cam. All he'd needed was a chance. Once he starting playing and excelling, he never quit. He had a stellar college career and was drafted into the pros. After a year, he'd left, and enlisted in the army. Everyone was shocked, except Dean.

Sarah had seen something in Cam that no one else had—character. The boy who was always fighting was now fighting for his country. But Dean worried about him being in Iraq. Cam was doing what he wanted, though, so Dean supported him wholeheartedly.

His eyes scanned the photo collage Claire had made of the girls' first birthdays. Other celebrations were there, too, but he couldn't take his eyes from that earliest one. Even though Claire had known very little about cooking, she'd insisted on baking Sarah's first birthday cake. He smiled at the lopsided concoction in the photo with its runny icing.

In the photo Sarah had cake and icing all over her. He and Claire were standing beside the high chair, staring into each other's eyes. Claire's hand rested on her protruding stomach; she was pregnant with Sami. They were happy. They were in love. Those days had been the hardest, but ironically, the happiest of their lives.

When they'd agreed to allow Robert and Gwen into their lives, it had been the right decision. But it hadn't been easy. The Thorntons had continually tried to manipulate Claire. They'd underestimated their daughter, though.

Sarah's Eighth Birthday

THE HOUSE WAS ALIVE with chattering, giggling little girls. While they played dress-up in Sarah's room, Dean and Claire got the breakfast room ready for cake, ice cream and gifts.

Gwen and Robert were visiting with Bunny in the den, but Dean's mom was doing most of the talking. The Thorntons were answering in monosyllables.

"It'll take time. They'll adjust," Claire whispered to Dean as they listened to the stilted conversation.

He nodded, but he had his doubts. Adjusting to the Thorntons was like trying to walk with a rock in your shoe. Any way you tried, it was going to be uncomfortable, and sometimes downright painful.

Gwen walked into the kitchen, followed by Robert. "Claire, darling, I hope you don't mind, but we bought Sarah a special gift."

Claire stopped stirring the punch. "What is it?"

"We had our jeweler design a small diamond ring for her."

"Excuse me?" Claire carefully placed the ladle on the counter. "You bought a diamond ring for an eight-year-old girl?"

"It didn't cost that much—"

"No. Absolutely not." She shook her head.

"That's not fair," Gwen said.

"I agree, Mom, it isn't fair that you spring this on us at the last minute, when I've told you no expensive gifts."

"I don't understand your objection." Gwen pursed her lips.

"She's eight years old and she'd lose it within the week."

"At that age you were good about taking care of your things." Robert had to have his say. "And I feel Sarah is a lot like you."

Claire didn't budge. "I said no. It's an inappropriate gift for a little girl."

"You're just trying to punish us," Gwen said in a petulant tone. "We hardly know our granddaughters and you won't allow them to visit us."

Dean felt Claire stiffen, and he knew he had to step in before the party went awry. "This is our daughter's birthday and around here it's always a happy day. No arguing or complaining—just happiness."

"I'm sorry," Robert said at once. "At times we feel left out, and I know that's our fault." He paused. "We'll take the ring back."

"But we don't have a gift for our granddaughter," Gwen wailed.

Claire walked to where the presents were arranged on the table, and picked up a small package. She handed it to her mother. "We've had her ears pierced, and these are some earrings she's been wanting. They're inexpensive and it doesn't matter if she loses them."

"Thank you," Gwen replied, tight-lipped.

"You can give her the ring when she's older."

"Thank you, darling," her mother repeated, but for some reason she just couldn't let it go. She stared at the cake Claire had made especially for Sarah, an elaborate, edible castle suitable for a princess. Claire had gotten very good at baking and decorating.

"I don't understand why you wouldn't let me bring the cake. Giorgio does such beautiful creations, and it would have saved you all that work in the kitchen."

Claire patiently laid pink napkins, spoons and forks on the table. "I make all the girls' birthday cakes and I enjoy doing it."

"Of course, dear," she remarked in that same tight voice.

"Come on, Gwen." Bunny joined the conversation. "Sit your butt in a chair and stop being so bitchy."

"I beg your pardon?" Gwen puffed out her chest. "I do not appreciate that kind of language."

"And I do not appreciate you nagging at my son and sweet Claire." Bunny met her stare with a glare of her own. "So sit your posterior down."

Before Dean could intervene, seven little girls came

charging into the room all dressed in princess attire and all talking at once. They stopped and oohed and ahhed over the cake.

The glow on Claire's face was worth putting up with Gwen.

Sami went to her mom. "I'm tired, Mommy."

At six, their daughter was still struggling with her injured leg. Claire picked her up and held her on her hip. Sami was too big for this, but they still pampered her.

Claire kissed her cheek. "You don't want to miss any of your sister's birthday."

Sami shook her head, staring at the gifts. "She has lots of presents."

Dean and Claire exchanged a glance. It wasn't about being tired. It was about all the gifts Sarah was getting.

"Just like you'll have in two months when you turn seven," Claire reminded her.

"Yeah." Sami immediately brightened. "How long is two months, Mommy?"

Claire kissed her again. "Not long, baby."

Sarah tore into her presents like a hurricane. When she got to the earrings, her mouth fell open and her eyes widened with excitement. "Just what I wanted." She ran to the Thorntons, hugging Robert and then Gwen. "Thank you. You're the best grandparents ever."

And just like that all was forgiven.

Until Sarah realized what she'd said. She stepped back, twisting her hands together. "I mean you're the best grandparents after Grandma Bunny. Bunny's my, well, my grandma."

"You got it, sugar." Bunny winked at her.

Gwen puffed up like a frog and stayed that way most

of the day. She relented when Sami let her hold her. It seemed to make up for Sarah's indiscretion.

DEAN REPLACED THE PHOTO, knowing those years hadn't been easy for them or the Thorntons. But against the odds, they became a family.

DARKNESS FELL and Claire wandered restlessly through the house, wishing with everything in her for that feeling she'd had at eighteen—a burning desire to be a mother. Nothing was standing in her way.

Not her parents.

Not her education.

Nothing.

She ran her hands through her hair, trying to feel all those emotions that made her Claire Rennels, mother. She felt nothing but resentment inside her. And she hated herself for that.

Suddenly she realized she was more than a mother. She was also a wife and a daughter. The daughter part was the hardest, but her parents were in her life, and she was grateful.

The early years had been a tug-of-war as her parents tried to exert their authority at every turn. It had all come to a head the summer of 1997. Her parents wanted to take the girls to Europe for a month. She and Dean had refused because their daughters had church camp, and Claire and Dean were two of the parent volunteers. Sarah also had cheerleading camp, and they'd arranged a family vacation to Disneyland. Their plans had all been made, but her parents were furious, saying they just didn't want the girls to go with them.

Gwen and Robert went alone, leaving for Europe without a word. They didn't call after that, and the girls missed them.

Claire did, too.

She wondered why they couldn't be a real family, loving and respectful of each other, but that seemed to be asking too much of her parents.

Claire didn't know how to resolve the situation. They'd come so far.

But sometimes life had a way of intervening.

Summer, 1997

CLAIRE FOLDED THE LAST of the laundry as Dean walked into the bedroom.

"Hey, beautiful." He kissed her over the laundry basket and stared into her solemn face. "Still no word from your parents, hmm?"

"No. It's been four weeks now and the girls keep asking."

"Honey…"

"I'm okay," she said. "I don't know why I expected them to respect my wishes."

He took the basket from her and placed it on the bed. "Let's go out to dinner. That might cheer you up. Where are the girls?"

"Sarah's spending the night with Paige and Sami's outside trying to teach Barney a new trick."

"Barney doesn't know any tricks. He just knows how to eat and sleep."

"But we love him anyway."

"Yes, we do." Dean slipped his arms around her waist. "And I love you. We're not leaving this room until I see you smile again."

"Dean…"

He twirled her around and they fell onto the bed, the laundry basket bouncing to the floor.

She laughed. She couldn't help it. Dean always had a way of making her laugh.

He held her face in his hands. "Honey, they're testing you."

"I know." She gently kissed him. "I just wish they didn't make everything so hard."

He groaned and captured her lips in a toe-curling kiss. All her worries floated away and she gave herself up to this man whom she loved more than anything.

"Gosh, are y'all at it again?" Sami said from the doorway.

"Yes." Dean replied without moving, his arms locked tight around Claire as she lay on top of him.

Barney barked and jumped onto the bed. Claire rose to her feet and straightened her blouse.

"It's not even dark yet." Sami walked farther into the room. "You guys are going to warp my mind."

Dean reached out and grabbed her, tickling her until she begged for mercy. Barney barked excitedly until he let go of her.

"Hey, munchkin?" Dean ruffled Sami's hair, which had come undone from her ponytail. "Want to go out for dinner?" He held up a finger. "And no pizza."

"Geez, Daddy, you take the fun out of everything."

He lifted an eyebrow. "Really?"

Sami shrugged, crawling from the bed. "That's kind of slang, you know, like you're a typical dad."

Dean frowned. "I don't have a clue what you girls are saying half the time."

"That's cool, Daddy. We don't want you to."

"And does Mommy understand?" he asked.

Claire leaned over and kissed his nose. "Mommy understands everything." She dragged out the last word, smiling.

"Yeah," Sami agreed. "It's kind of hard to sneak anything past Mommy. It's like Grandma Bunny says. Mommy knows us inside and out, upside down and sideways, and some stuff even we don't know about."

"Well, I'm glad someone's on duty." Dean got to his feet. "So what's it going to be for dinner, ladies?"

"Barney and I want to go to Grandma Bunny's and spend the night," Sami informed them. "We'll have popcorn and *pizza*—" she emphasized the last word dramatically "—and watch a movie until I fall asleep. Bunny times me. I fell asleep at one-sixteen last time. I'm aiming for one-thirty."

Dean looked at Claire.

"Since it's Saturday, it's okay by me," she said. "But phone Bunny first."

"I already did," Sami called over her shoulder as she exited the room. Suddenly she stopped and glanced back. "Has Gigi or Grandpa called?"

"No, sweetie," Claire replied, getting annoyed that her parents were doing this to her daughters.

"When will they be back?"

"I don't know."

Sami frowned. "Don't they miss us?" Before Claire could find a suitable reply, she added, "I miss them."

There was a long pause and Claire was at a loss for words—the correct words.

Dean saved the moment. "Tomorrow, when you get back from Bunny's and Sarah comes home, we'll call Gigi and Grandpa to check if they're home, so we can visit. How's that?"

"Cool, Daddy." Sami was happy again and bounded out of the room, Barney loping after her.

"Thank you," Claire said, and went into his arms.

"It's time to put a stop to this. It's also time for Dad to stop being superficial around here," Dean replied, tongue in cheek.

"He's not superficial to me." Claire nuzzled against his body. "Let's go eat at that little Italian place you like. We'll celebrate you being named the new high school football coach and athletic director."

"We're starting a new era."

"You've earned it. Although Sarah's not happy her dad is now going to be at the high school, watching her every move." Claire ran her fingers through his hair. "But deep down I know she's proud of you. *I* certainly am."

His eyes gleamed. "Tonight you can show me how proud."

A bubble of laughter left her throat. "Oh, yes. We'll have wine and sit close together and come home and..."

"And what?" He grinned.

"Get really close together."

"Sounds like my kind of plan." His grin widened.

Almost two hours later they came through their back door arm in arm. Claire had had two glasses of wine and was feeling a little tipsy. Or it could be the handsome man on her arm and that light in his eyes.

"Do you hear that?" he asked as they walked into the den.

"No." She listened closely. "I don't hear a thing."

"I don't, either. We're actually alone."

She raised an eyebrow. "And what are we going to do about it?"

His hand went to the zipper on her dress. "Get naked and nasty."

"Dean," she screeched, and ran into the bedroom.

He caught her and they tumbled onto the bed in a fit of laughter. With sighs and moans, they pulled off their clothes.

The ringing of the phone pierced the moment.

"Leave it," Dean said, his lips blazing a trail to her breasts.

She was so tempted, but responsibility came with being a parent. "It could be about the girls," she breathed as his mouth found her nipple.

Dean sagged back on the pillow. "Hurry."

She reached for the phone. "Hello."

"Claire, this is your mother." There was a long pause. "Your father's had a heart attack."

CHAPTER ELEVEN

A CHILL RAN THROUGH Claire and she thought she was going to faint.

"What?" she managed to ask.

"Your father has had a massive heart attack. They're taking him into surgery now. We're at the Heart Hospital. Please, Claire, I need you."

"I'll be right there." She dropped the phone and started grabbing her clothes from the floor.

Dean replaced the receiver. "Honey, what is it?"

She kept getting dressed. She had to hurry.

He caught her hands and she realized she was trembling. "Honey?"

She stared down at his strong fingers. "Daddy...Daddy had a heart attack." She gulped back a sob. "I have to go."

They dressed hurriedly and within minutes were speeding toward the hospital. Claire felt frozen inside, though the temperature was in the high nineties. All she could think was that her father was going to die, and the last time she had seen him they'd parted in anger. A sob clogged her throat.

Dean reached out and took her hand. She clutched his tightly, feeling his warmth, his strength. "Honey, relax," he said gently.

"I can't. I just keep thinking…"

"Don't." He squeezed her fingers. "They do amazing things with surgery these days. Let's just wait until we get there."

He pulled into the parking lot and they bolted for the entrance. Claire had forgotten to ask where her father was, but Dean found out quickly. They hurried to the surgery floor. When Claire saw her mother, she stopped short and Dean bumped into her. His hands gripped her elbows, and she was glad, because her knees suddenly felt like rubber.

Her mother sat all alone in a waiting room, wiping at her eyes. In that moment Claire realized just how alone her parents were. Her dad had a brother who had died in Vietnam, her mom a sister who'd been killed in an auto accident in her twenties. They had no other close relatives.

Just Claire.

The guilt was suddenly suffocating.

Dean nudged her forward, and she walked to her mother and sat beside her. Gwen threw herself at Claire and sobbed like a baby on her shoulder.

Claire realized she was crying, too, and she couldn't seem to stop.

Dean sat next to Gwen and looped his arm across the back of her chair, his hand rubbing Claire's arm. Claire felt his touch, and strength suddenly suffused her. She drew a ragged breath. "Mom, shh."

Gwen raised her head and dabbed at her eyes. "I'm so afraid," she mumbled.

"I'm here now and we'll face this together. Has the doctor said anything?"

"He said he'd talk to me after the surgery."

"Then we'll wait." Claire settled back, brushing away another tear.

"Thank you, darling. I just couldn't face this alone."

"Since you have a daughter, son-in-law and grand-daughters, you don't have to," Dean said.

"I appreciate that, Dean."

"How did it happen?" Claire asked.

"We went out to eat at the club, and Robert ordered the prime rib, as he always does. I've told him many times he needs to change his diet, but he never listens to me. When we got home, he wasn't feeling well. We were supposed to play bridge with the Carlsons but he didn't feel like going so I canceled."

Gwen took a breath. "He threw up about nine, and we thought something might have been wrong with the food he ate. But then his chest started hurting and his arm went numb. I called 911 immediately. He was feeling so bad he didn't object." She fingered her pearls. "Everything happened so fast after that. It was like a nightmare."

Claire put an arm around her. "Daddy's a strong man. I'm hoping for the best."

"Me, too, but his diet is atrocious and his only exercise is golf."

"We'll work on that." Claire handed her mom another tissue. "When did you get back from Europe?"

Gwen dabbed at her eyes again. "We never went."

"What?"

"We've been there many times and we were looking forward to taking the girls. Without them it wouldn't have been much fun."

Claire shook her head, feeling resentment gathering force inside her.

Dean came to the rescue. "Gwen, this has to stop. You can't keep manipulating us and expecting to get your way. Next time we need more notice."

His mother-in-law's eyes opened wide. "You mean you would have let them go?"

"Of course."

"We thought you just didn't want them with us."

"You didn't give us a chance to offer a compromise," he told her. "You just got angry and left. Claire and I are not happy you've upset the girls."

Gwen straightened. "They're upset?"

"Yes. They miss you."

"They do?"

"Mom, why is that so hard for you to believe?" Claire asked. "You've been in the girls' lives for a while now. Not a day goes by that one of them doesn't ask when you're coming back. And you've been home the whole time. I'm sorry, but that upsets me."

"I'm a foolish old woman," Gwen moaned.

Time wore on as they rehashed the problem, needing to hear and say things that had been left unspoken.

"Where are the girls?" Gwen finally asked.

"Sarah's at a friend's and Sami's at Bunny's."

"They stay with Bunny a lot."

"Yes," Claire said. "They love her, just like they love you."

Gwen hiccupped. "I wish they were here. I know that's not appropriate, but I just love looking at them. They're so beautiful, polite and respectful. You've done a great job raising them."

"Thank you, Mother. That means a lot to me."

Gwen looked at her son-in-law. "You're a fine young man, Dean. I wish I had seen that years ago."

He took Gwen's hand and squeezed it. She squeezed back, and Claire wanted to burst into tears all over again. This was a happy moment, though. Her mother had finally accepted Dean.

Claire didn't give herself time to rejoice, but she held on to the memory.

It seemed like forever, but suddenly the doctor, still in his scrubs, appeared in the doorway. They got to their feet, Claire and Dean on either side of Gwen, holding her hands.

"Mrs. Thornton," Dr. Meadows said, and looked at Claire and Dean.

"This is my daughter, Claire, and my son-in-law."

The doctor nodded.

"How is my husband?"

"He's in recovery. We did a triple bypass and he came through the surgery very well. If he follows new guidelines for diet and lifestyle, I'm expecting a full recovery."

"Oh, thank God." Gwen's knees buckled and Dean held her up. "When can I see him?"

"They'll have him in the cardiac care unit in about an hour. Please keep your visits short. He needs to rest and heal now."

"We'll do that. And we'll take very good care of him."

The doctor nodded and walked out.

Claire hugged her mother and Dean wrapped his arms around both women. It was a healing moment for all of them.

The waiting wouldn't be so bad now. Her father was going to be okay.

When they were finally able to visit him, he was unconscious. As Claire walked into the unit, memories of Sami's stay in the hospital suddenly gripped her. She felt a moment of panic and quickly forced it away.

She focused on her father instead, and the knowledge that he was going to be fine. They weren't going to lose him.

But she hardly recognized the man in the bed attached to machines. He looked old. When had his hair turned so white? She and Dean sat by his bedside, the only sounds the beeping of the monitors.

As she looked at him, she noticed the wrinkles, too. He'd gotten older right before her eyes. She stared at him, remembering so much of her childhood... Riding on his shoulders, feeling safe and secure, knowing her daddy would never drop her. Waiting patiently as he put training wheels on her bike, then trusting that she wouldn't fall, because her daddy was watching her. He was always there to protect her, but somewhere in her teens, things had changed. He'd become overprotective and stern, unwilling to let her have a say in her own life.

As an adult she recognized his actions for what they were—fear. Fear of his little girl growing up and away from him. He'd been afraid she wouldn't make the right choices, so he'd tried to make them for her. Stroking his hand, she acknowledged having those feelings herself now, as a parent.

She'd resolved not to make those same mistakes with her daughters. Sarah was taking an interest in boys, and Claire and Dean encouraged her to talk about her friends. When she showed an interest in a boy who didn't meet with their approval, they didn't criticize. They'd learned their lesson with Cam, and they always kept the lines of communication open.

Claire's parents had their own way of dealing with situations, though. It seemed wrong to her, but she knew they were getting a second chance. And she was happy about that.

THE NEXT DAY her father was awake and asking for Claire. She and Dean had never left the hospital, and when the nurse came to get her, she wanted him to go with her. But she needed to speak to her father alone, he said, and she agreed. As Claire left the waiting room, she glanced back to see Gwen and Dean engrossed in conversation.

Things were definitely changing.

She walked into the CCU with a feeling of anticipation. Her father was in a room monitored by hospital staff at all times. The nurse's station was right outside the open door.

Claire spoke to the nurse and walked to her father's bedside His eyes were closed and he looked so frail, his skin ashen. Some of the monitors had been removed, but one was still attached to his heart, and an IV was in his arm. The man she'd always thought of as strong was now weak. She felt a catch in her throat.

She started to sit in the one available chair, but he opened his eyes. "Cl-aire," he murmured.

"It's okay, Daddy." She patted his arm. "Don't talk. Save your strength."

"I-lo-ve-you." His voice was low and broken, but she heard him.

Tears filled her eyes. Three little words, and they had the most amazing healing power. She leaned over and hugged him gently. "I love you, too."

"Gi-rls," he managed to say.

"They're fine and they'll be up to see you soon."

Satisfied, he drifted back to sleep, and after a while Claire went back to Dean. "How was it?" he asked, stroking her hair.

"He...he just wanted to tell me he loved me." She was unable to stop the tears that rolled from her eyes.

"Honey…" He took her in his arms and she rested against him.

"Where's Mom?" she asked at last.

"I made her go to the cafeteria to get something to eat."

Claire drew back. "And she listened to you?"

"You bet. We have a whole new understanding now." He cupped her face and ran his thumb over her cheek. "Of course, tomorrow could be a different story."

Claire shook her head. "I think things are changing for the better. At least we're talking, and for once my mother is listening."

"Communication is the key to every problem."

She smiled for the first time in twenty-four hours. "I thought it was a good defense."

"That, too." He pulled her to his side. "And a good offense."

"Dad asked about the girls. We have to tell them."

Dean glanced at his watch. "Sarah should be home in an hour, and I told Mom we'd call her before we picked up Sami."

"Did Bunny tell her?"

"No. You know Bunny. That's our job."

"She's right." Claire took Dean's hand and they walked down the hall. "Let's find Mom and let her know we're going to tell the girls."

An hour later they sat in the den with their daughters. The girls looked at them with confused expressions. Sarah's hair was in a French braid down her back, and her fingernails and toenails were a bright candy-apple red. It took Claire a moment to get used to that. Clearly, she'd had a good time at her friend Paige's.

She stood by Dean's chair, waiting for him to find the right words.

The girls weren't good at waiting.

Sami frowned. "You aren't going to give us the sex talk again, are you? I mean, boys are like aliens to me. Of course, they're like Velcro to Sarah."

Sarah jabbed her in the ribs with her elbow. "They are not."

"Oh yeah," Sami shot back. "You'd like to be stuck to Kyle Hornby."

"Shut up," her sister shouted.

"Stop it," Dean ordered, and his tone of voice got their attention. "Your mother and I have something to tell you."

They sobered instantly, knowing at once something was wrong. Sami got up and crawled onto Dean's lap as if she were six years old. Claire sat by Sarah and put an arm around her.

"What is it?" Sarah asked in a little-girl voice.

Dean wrapped his arms tight around Sami. "Your grandfather's had a heart attack."

"No!" Sami cried, and buried her face in his neck.

"Is he…? Is he…?" Sarah couldn't even make herself say the words.

Claire pulled her closer. "He's going to be fine, sweetie. He had a triple bypass last night and the doctor said he should make a full recovery."

"Oh, boy." Sami jumped off her dad's lap. "Let's go visit him. I know he'll want to see us."

Dean caught her hand. "Sweetie, he's in the cardiac care unit, and can only see visitors like Gigi at certain hours. I'm not sure they'll let you in."

"But we're his granddaughters."

"They have very strict rules, sweetheart."

All of a sudden Sarah broke into sobs.

"What is it?" Claire asked, holding her close.

"It's all our fault, 'cause we couldn't go on that trip with them."

Sami sank down beside them and both girls bawled like babies. "Girls, it's not your fault," Claire told them. "Grandpa has some bad eating habits and he needs to exercise more."

"We'll make sure he does that." Sarah raised her head, swiping her arm across her eyes.

Dean rose to his feet. "In the meantime, I'm sure Gigi would be happy to see you both."

In a flash the girls were on their feet and running for the car.

CHAPTER TWELVE

DEAN TOOK A SHOWER and prepared for bed. Tomorrow was another rigorous practice day. He and his assistant coaches were getting the team ready for their first game of the season. Justin Holcomb had turned into a talented quarterback, and Dean was counting on him not only to take the team to the state championship, but to win it.

The kid had an arm like Dean hadn't seen in a while. It reminded him of Troy Aikman's. Justin was big like Troy, too, and good at scrambling in the pocket. It took a hard hit to bring him down.

The state championship.

Coaching college football.

His dreams were within his grasp. How bad did he want them?

He picked up the wedding photos on the nightstand. Two pictures of Claire and him, side by side in a dark wood frame. The one on the left was from the day they'd married the first time, the other when they'd renewed their vows on their fifteenth wedding anniversary.

In the first photo they looked like the kids they'd been—two frightened teenagers. Bunny had taken the picture with her cheap camera, but it captured them perfectly.

They'd waited until after high school graduation to get

married. Claire wore a silky white, loose dress that fell to her ankles. Her long hair hung down her back. She held a bouquet of tiny white roses and baby's breath Bunny had bought for her.

Dean stood proudly in the suit he wore to church, and he remembered holding Claire's hand and feeling how cold it was. He'd brought it to his lips and kissed it. She'd smiled. In that moment he knew they were going to be okay.

Were they going to be okay now? He really needed to know that.

He glanced at the other picture, which evoked a completely different feeling. They'd been happy and it showed in their smiles. Claire wore an off-the-shoulder ivory gown that made her look gorgeous. Her blond hair was up and wispy strands teased her face, making her appear as young as Sarah.

Dean stood beside her in a tuxedo and a smile as wide as Texas.

Sitting on the bed now, he cradled the pictures against his chest as he remembered how that second wedding had come about.

Summer, 1997

ROBERT RECOVERED QUICKLY from his heart attack. Claire and Gigi sat with him around the clock, taking turns so that one was always with him. On the weekends Dean gave them a break.

One Saturday morning he went in early so Claire could spend some time with the girls and Gigi could sleep late. Claire was folding a blanket as he arrived. When she saw him, she went into his arms and kissed him.

"Morning," she whispered.

He just held her, because he knew how traumatic this was for her. She was trying so hard and he worried about her.

Robert was sitting up in bed, drinking juice. His color was so much better. "Morning, Dean."

"Good morning. How are you today?"

"A whole lot better. I'm alive and my daughter's with me."

Dean tried not to be resentful, because the man had been through a tremendous ordeal. But sometimes it wasn't easy to push down those old feelings.

Robert set his glass on a tray. "You know, Dean, I've hated you for a lot of years."

"Daddy."

"Sorry, sweetheart. I have something to say and I'm going to say it."

"Daddy, please."

"Let him talk, Claire. We need to get everything out into the open." Dean had a pretty good idea of where Robert was headed, so he sat in a chair and waited. He felt as if a hundred-yard pass was spiraling his way and if he caught it, he was going to win the game. If he dropped it, his life would be forever different.

"I never thought you were good enough for my daughter."

"I know that. And you might be surprised to know sometimes I don't think I'm good enough, either."

"You took her from us and our lives were empty."

"That was your choice, sir."

"She was my little girl. Why couldn't you have left her alone?"

If Dean were younger, the question would have made him very angry. But he was a parent now and knew exactly what Robert was feeling—that he'd taken advantage of Claire.

"Because I loved her."

"And I loved him," Claire said. "Looking back, I see how young we were, and I'm always amazed at how sure we were of that love, especially when everyone said it wouldn't last."

"In the early days, did you ever think of coming home?" Robert asked.

She shook her head. "No. But there were days I cried and wanted my parents."

"Oh, sweetheart, I'm so sorry." He held out a hand and she took it. "I just couldn't get past you choosing Dean over us."

"I loved Dean and I was pregnant with his child. There was no way I'd ever leave him."

"For once in my life I wish I had listened to your mother. She wanted me to give in and accept Dean. When I refused, she said I'd lost my mind, and I believe she was right." He smoothed the sheet with his fingers. "I'll never forgive myself for not being there for you when Sarah and Sami were born."

"You're in their lives now, Daddy, and we can only try to make things better."

"You're right, sweetheart." Robert looked at Dean. "You're a talented coach and an honorable man. You've taken very good care of my daughter and granddaughters. I'm very appreciative."

"Thank you, sir." Dean stood and held out his hand. "To a new beginning."

Robert shook it, his tired brown eyes looking directly at him. "It's nothing against you personally, but you'll never be good enough for my little girl."

"Daddy!"

Dean held up a palm. "It's all right. I know exactly how Robert feels. No guy on this planet is ever going to be good enough for *my* girls."

"You're right about that." Robert nodded. "But I guess we'll have to learn to be more tolerant."

"Yeah." Dean rocked back on his heels. "It might take some practice, though."

"Is this some sort of male bonding?" Claire asked.

"Sort of." Robert took a deep breath. "I am sorry for what I put you young people through."

"Let's just concentrate on the future," she said.

"I always dreamed of walking my little girl down the aisle, and Gwen has fantasized about Claire's wedding almost since the day she was born," Robert told Dean.

"We can't change that, Daddy. I'm sorry."

There was a long pause. Then Robert said, "You could get married again."

She looked at Dean and he gazed back at her, but neither had anything to say.

"You'll be married fifteen years in May. You could renew your vows and give your mother that chance to plan your wedding. We wouldn't do anything elaborate, just something elegant with family and friends—in our home. You always said you wanted to get married in the gazebo."

"I'd forgotten that," Claire murmured, a light in her eyes Dean hadn't seen before. A light created by dreams, wishes and fairy tales. A light often found in the eyes of young girls.

Dean walked around the bed and took her hand. "Claire Rennels, will you marry me again?"

The light became blinding. "Yes, yes." She threw herself into his arms.

The Wedding, May 30, 1998

THE GIRLS AND GIGI planned the wedding for nine months. Claire made the decision about her dress, but other than that she gave her mother carte blanche.

Dean realized a big wedding wasn't something Claire really wanted, but for her parents she went along with the plan. At least that was one less thing he didn't have to feel guilty about, or one less thing he hadn't been able to give her. Back then they'd only needed each other. That hadn't changed.

The big day was something they would never forget. The Thorntons' two-story Tudor was decorated inside and out. White carpet trailed from the patio to the gazebo, with white chairs placed in rows on both sides. The girls had tied big white net bows on the aisle chairs and flowers seemed to be everywhere.

Tables with white linens and more flowers were arranged around the pool for the catered meal. A band played softly in the background.

Claire had spent the night with her parents for the first time in fifteen years. The girls stayed, too. Dean was home alone. He wasn't crazy about that, but the moment he saw Claire coming down the carpet on Robert's arm, he forgot everything but her.

All he could think was how much he loved her.

How much he would always love her.

After the gourmet meal, they danced, and their feet never seemed to touch the floor.

Dean gazed into her face. "Happy?"

"Very," she murmured, her eyes sparkling.

He kissed her briefly. "I missed you last night."

"I learned something last night."

"What?"

"That I'm not a girl anymore. I'm all grown up and I need my husband at night."

He grinned, realizing how much he needed her to say that. "I can't wait to remove that gown."

"I can't wait for you to, either." She laughed and he laughed with her.

They danced until after midnight, and then a limo took them to a hotel, where they stayed for only a few hours. Their plane left for Paris at five forty-five and they made it just in time. They spent eight days strolling the tree-lined Champs-Élysées with other lovers. Claire was fascinated with the Louvre and Dean got caught up in her excitement over the paintings by the masters, the other art treasures and the sculptures.

The Eiffel Tower was another favorite. The lacing together of spidery, wrought-iron bridge pylons was a marvel to see. Touring the historical chateaus and vineyards, and eating French cuisine, were incredible experiences.

They were young again and in love, and they enjoyed every minute of the honeymoon they'd never had. But they were ready to go when the day came to board the plane for home.

The girls had spent that time in Europe with their grandparents. Dean and Claire were home five days when their daughters returned. They'd never been apart that long, and as he hugged Sarah, Sami and Claire in one big embrace, Dean knew they had made all the right choices for all the right reasons.

DEAN PLACED THE PHOTO back on the nightstand. He ran both hands through his hair and stared at their king-size bed. For twenty-five years they'd slept spoon fashion; Claire's back was always curved into his chest. He was used to having her in his arms and wasn't sure he could sleep without her.

Not ready to brave the night, he headed for his study, planning to put Bunny's inspired idea of making Claire feel young again into action. Grabbing pen and paper, he began to write. *"My sweet Claire…"*

CLAIRE WOKE UP on the sofa again, still in her clothes. She had to stop this, but also knew why she didn't climb into bed when she was tired. She didn't like sleeping without Dean's arms around her.

Then go home, a voice whispered inside her head. *Go home and face your future.*

The thought was interrupted by the roll of her stomach. Ten minutes later, she sat on the bathroom floor gazing at her chipped pink toenails, waiting for her stomach to settle down.

She wondered if she had any nail polish remover here. And what did it matter? Resting her head against the wall, she tried to figure out once again what was really bothering her.

What was at the center of her heartache? *She'd screwed up.* There it was—the truth that was disabling her. Her parents were so proud of her decision to go back to school. How was she going to tell them about the pregnancy?

She opened her eyes. Since Sarah worked in her dad's law office, they probably already knew. No, they'd gone to Dallas for the weekend to visit an old law buddy of Robert's. Claire had forgotten that for a moment.

Once again they would be disappointed in her. Once

again she would make her own choices, though. She just wished she had the strength to handle this pregnancy like she should, and to stop searching for excuses.

And she wished she had the strength to get up off the floor.

After a moment she felt better and climbed to her feet. In the closet she found cleaning supplies and scrubbed the commode, and then she stripped and took a shower.

After dressing in shorts and a tank top, she headed for the kitchen. She made dry toast and resisted the urge to make coffee. Maybe half a cup, she told herself as she reached for the pot.

She heard a tap on the glass, a key in the lock, and turned to see Sami coming through the door.

CHAPTER THIRTEEN

"SAMI, WHAT ARE YOU DOING here?"

She held up a bag. "I brought breakfast."

"Don't you have to teach this morning?"

Sami set the sack on the table. "I don't have an early class today, so I thought I'd come and have breakfast with my mother."

"But you still have to be at school."

Sami ignored her, pulling items out of the bag. "I brought bear claws and lattes. Yours is mostly milk."

"Oh, bless you." Claire couldn't help but smile. "I needed this." And she hoped her stomach did, too.

They sat at the table and Claire sipped her latte. It was heavenly, even though it had a strong milk flavor.

Sami pulled off a piece of bear claw and popped it into her mouth. "Do you remember when you used to bribe me with these when I was in the hospital in Houston?"

"Yes." Claire broke off a section and nibbled on it, testing her stomach. "But I'm surprised you remembered that. You were only four."

"I know," Sami murmured.

"You turned four right after the accident. We had a makeshift party at the hospital. You'd just woken up and weren't in a mood to celebrate, not even when your father showed you the shoes with the rhinestones on them."

"I don't remember that birthday. I only remember bits and pieces of that time, but I'll never forget you getting me hooked on this sweet pastry."

"You were getting so thin and the doctor said to let you eat anything you wanted. I found bear claws in the cafeteria and bought one, mostly for me, but when you wanted it, I gave it to you. You ate the whole thing and bear claws became a big part of your diet."

"I still love them." Sami took a sip of her mocha frappuccino with a shot of caramel. "So how are you?"

Claire looked into her daughter's brown eyes, so like her own. "I'm okay."

She shifted nervously. "Then why aren't you home with Daddy?"

"Sweetie, I need some time, that's all."

Sami twisted her cup. "I remember one night when I was in the hospital, waking up and finding you crying. I asked why. Do you recall what you said?"

Claire placed her cup on the table. "Sami, you can't possibly remember that."

Her daughter stared straight at her. "You said you missed Daddy."

Claire was stunned. How could she remember? It had been the Valentine's Day Claire had written Dean a letter, tears streaming down her face as she had poured out her thoughts.

"Yes, I did say that, and you said you missed Daddy, too, so we decided to call him. But before we could, he walked in."

Sami nodded. "It was like a miracle." She continued

to fiddle with her cup. "Why don't you need Daddy now?"

Claire suddenly knew what the visit was about. Samantha was afraid her parents were separating.

"Sami, sweetie, your dad and I are fine. I'm just having a hard time dealing with a pregnancy at my age."

Her daughter leaned forward. "Don't listen to Sarah. She always has her head in the clouds. I think it's cool you and Dad are still doing it."

Still doing it. How old did Sami think they were?

Despite herself, Claire smiled. "We'll have this conversation when you're married and forty-three. You can tell me how old you feel."

"Mom! I didn't mean it like that." Sami gathered the napkins, stuffed them into the bag and carried it to the trash. "Besides, I don't think I'll ever get married."

That shook Claire. "Why would you say that?"

Sami shrugged. "You and Daddy have this perfect marriage, and there's not another guy like him out there—just gigantic egos walking around who act like jerks."

Claire got up and put her arm around her daughter. Together they walked into the den and sat on the sofa. Sarah had been the one who had endless dates come through their home, much to the detriment of Dean's blood pressure. Sami wasn't as popular. It wasn't that she wasn't asked out, but she had a way of putting off the boys.

In high school Sarah had been a cheerleader. Sami chose not to try out for the honor. She was obsessed with tennis and gave it her all. In college, Sarah joined Gwen's old sorority. Again, it wasn't Sami's thing, but Sarah bugged her until she joined. Sami didn't participate like Sarah wanted her to, and they argued a lot about it. Then they compromised. Sarah played tennis and Sami joined the parties and the sisterhood.

Sami preferred to avoid social gatherings, though—and men. Claire knew it was because of her leg, and the scars that no one noticed but her. Sami carefully protected herself.

And her heart.

Claire feared her daughter was doing that now.

"This is more about your leg, isn't it?"

"Maybe." That stubborn chin jutted out, just like Dean's.

Claire stroked her arm, as she had so many times when Sami was a child. "What happened?"

Sami rested her head on her mom's shoulder. "You know I was dating David."

"Yes, the baseball coach."

"He pursued me. I didn't go after him. He seemed like a really nice guy, and I finally agreed to go out with him. We've been dating for three months now, so I thought it was time to tell him about my leg. I told him about the accident, the surgeries, and how you and Daddy fought to make sure I'd have a normal life." Sami rubbed her head against Claire. "He had one question."

She drew a long breath. "What was it?"

"Would I be able to have children?"

"Sami, baby…" Claire closed her eyes, feeling her child's pain. The removal of one of Sami's ovaries didn't make conceiving a baby impossible. It just made it difficult, especially with her injured hip.

"I told him what the doctor told us—that I might not be able to." Sami raised her head. "I haven't heard from him in days, so it's safe to say the relationship is over."

"Oh, honey." Claire cupped Sami's face in both her

hands. "I fought like hell for you to have a normal life, and if I have to drag every eligible bachelor in Texas to your door, you're going to have a husband and a family."

Sami grinned. "That sounds sort of like Gigi."

Claire hugged her daughter, knowing those protective motherly instincts were strong in her. And she had never acknowledged it before, but her mother had had those same instincts when Claire got pregnant at age eighteen. Unlike Gwen, though, she would support Sami in all her decisions.

Claire drew back and looked into Sami's eyes. "That is, if you want a husband and family."

"I'm not sure what I want." She tucked her hair behind her ear. "All I know is that I want a love like yours and Daddy's." Sami pulled away. "And why are we talking about me? I'm worried about you two."

"We're fine."

"I don't understand why you have to stay here by yourself."

"Sweetie, your father and I are not getting a divorce, if that's what you're worried about. As I told you, I'm trying to adjust to a very difficult situation."

"I'll help," Sami said earnestly. "I'll move back home and help take care of the baby, especially on the weekends."

"Listen to me," Claire said just as earnestly. "You're not moving home because of the baby. Go to work and I'll call you later. And stop worrying."

She didn't budge. "What about college?"

"Sami…"

"It's because of Sarah and me that you didn't go in the first place."

"Sweetie, this isn't about you or Sarah."

Sami looked directly at her. "But it is, especially me. I

know you took a job as a teacher's aide to be there for me when I fell."

Claire just hugged her child tighter. Sami had fallen a lot. The kids teased her and called her Slippery Sami. They weren't kind. But once Claire got involved with the class and began to know the children, she made sure that behavior stopped. Sami grew stronger, more confident, and made friends.

"All those years, you and Daddy went to tournaments with me when you didn't have to. No one else's parents went, especially in college. Those times Daddy couldn't go because of football, you were always there. I know you were worried in case I fell and couldn't get up." Sami looked down at her hands. "And I didn't have the courage to tell you I didn't need you, because I did. I needed you there to pick me up." Sami glanced at her mother. "But I don't anymore. You've made me strong and independent, and I can now pick myself up and take care of jerks like David."

Claire touched her daughter's face. "I know you can."

"Sarah and I never realized it before, but our educations cost plenty and kept you from going to college."

"Sami, baby." Claire gathered her child into her arms again. "Stop trying to take the blame for something that was completely out of your control. It was my life and my choices, and I did everything out of my deep love for you and Sarah."

"But I want to help now."

"I know you do, and that means the world to me. I love you all the more for the offer." She kissed Sami's forehead. "I want you to go on with your life and find the perfect Prince Charming who will sweep you off your feet and be there to pick you up when you need help."

"Haven't you heard they're all frogs?"

"Sweetie, that's very cynical."

Sami frowned. "You keep bringing the conversation back to me."

Claire gave her a squeeze. "Go to work and stop worrying. I love you."

There was silence for a moment.

"Mom?"

"What?"

"Please go to college."

"I'll think about it."

They hugged tightly and she reluctantly left for work.

Sami was a worrier. She'd been that way even before the accident, which exacerbated the trait. Sami liked to know what was going to happen before it happened.

But life wasn't like that.

Claire did enough worrying for them both, and she prayed her daughter found the right man to love her just the way she was. Sami had so many wonderful qualities, and there had to be a man out there who would recognize and cherish the sweet, compassionate, intelligent and spunky young woman she was.

CLAIRE DROVE to the convenience store for milk and couldn't resist buying candy bars and ice cream. She suddenly had a craving for butter pecan.

As she drove back, she thought about Sami and the competitive nature she'd inherited from her father. Sometimes Claire had thought that would be the death of her, having to watch her daughter put herself through so much misery just to win. Looking back, she knew it was much more. Sami had to prove she was just as good as a healthy person. Claire remembered one time in particular when she and Dean had had words because he encouraged Sami to push herself. Claire was more worried about Sami's health.

Spring 2001 State Championship, Houston, Texas

CLAIRE AND DEAN sat courtside, watching Sami as she focused on the game. The playoffs had been rigorous and she was tired, but there was no way Claire could make her stop now. Sami was facing Brooke Beckham from Dallas for the championship.

Sami won the first set 6-3, but was defeated in the second 7-6, in a heartbreaking loss in the tie breaker. In the third and deciding set the game was at deuce, and Sami was serving for the match.

She glanced at Dean and he nodded. They had secret signals. Sami trusted her coach, Ellen Simmons, but she trusted her father more. Claire just wanted the game over. Her stomach was in a huge knot.

Sami drove a top-spin serve and the ball landed in the far corner and spun out. Brooke managed to slam it down the line. Sami read it perfectly and sprinted toward the ball. She lunged a forehand crosscourt, but as her racquet met the ball her leg gave way. Her body crashed to the court. The ball hit the top of the net and fell on Brooke's side for a winner.

"Advantage Rennels," the chair umpire said.

The crowd clapped, and then suddenly there was complete silence as they realized Sami wasn't getting up.

Claire and Dean were instantly on their feet. Claire reached her first and fell down by her daughter. Sami lay prone and breathing heavily.

"Baby, Mommy's here," Claire said, and the car accident was so vivid in her mind that chills popped up on her skin.

Dean knelt on her other side. "Sweetie, are you hurt?"

"Daddy," she moaned. "Get me up, please."

"Sami, are you hurt?" he repeated.

Ellen walked out to see if Sami could continue to play.

"Daddy, get me up."

Dean lifted her into a sitting position. "If you're hurt, Sami, you have to quit. There's no shame in losing when you've done your very best."

"Should we forfeit?" Ellen asked.

"No," Sami shouted. "I can finish. I just need a minute."

"Baby…" Claire stroked her sweaty hair. "It's okay to quit. You—"

"Don't baby me, Mom, not now."

That hurt Claire's feelings, but she put it down to Sami's competitive spirit. The mother in her just didn't understand it, though. She wanted Sami to stop now, before she injured herself badly.

Dean glanced at Claire and she sent him a clear message with her eyes. *Make her stop.*

"Sami, I want to know if you're injured," he said.

"I'm tired, Daddy, that's all. My leg gave way."

"Can you get up?"

Sami winced. "If you help me."

"This is ridiculous." Claire couldn't stop herself, she was so worried.

"Mom, Dad, please," Sami begged. "I'm one point away from winning. I worked all season for this. Please don't make me stop. I can do it."

"Dean, I'm not sure about this." Ellen said.

Dean stared at their daughter, and Claire knew he would be the one to make the final decision. Not Sami. Not Claire. But Dean.

Sami knew it, too.

Claire held her breath as she waited for him to say the right words.

"I can do this, Daddy. I can. Please."

Hearing the entreaty in Sami's voice, Claire had no doubt what Dean was going to do. At that moment she hated sports and everything about it.

He put his arm around Sami's waist and lifted her to her feet. "Try your legs. Can you stand without pain?"

"The chair umpire wants to know if Sami can continue," Ellen said.

"Yes. I just need a minute," she replied.

"This is it," her coach told her. "You're out of minutes. You play or forfeit. I'll leave that decision up to you and your father. Either way, you're still a winner to me."

"Thank you." Sami tested her leg, walking slowly back and forth. "I'm playing."

"Okay." Dean caught her shoulders and made Sami look at him. "Use a slice serve to her backhand. Aim for the outside corner and make it count, Sami. You have to make it count."

"I know, Daddy." She drew in a deep breath.

"Dean…"

He took Claire's arm and led her from the court. "She has to do this, Claire. Please understand that."

"I only understand that my child is hurt."

"Let's don't argue." He reached for her hand and held it tight. Neither took a breath as they waited for Sami to serve. Everyone was on their feet. Sarah had come out of the stands to be with them.

Brooke danced from one foot to the other, waiting for the serve. Sami was barely standing.

Claire closed her eyes. She couldn't watch. Then she quickly opened them. She had to watch. Sami might need her.

Almost in slow motion, Sami threw the ball up, and her racket connected with a loud thud. The serve was so fast Claire barely saw it. Brooke made a dive for the ball, but it was gone.

Sami won.

Dean sprinted to catch her before she fell to the court, but with a burst of energy Sami leaped into his arms.

"I told you I could do it. I told you," she cried against his shoulder.

Claire stood there, tears of joy streaming down her cheeks, wondering how she managed to live with two such competitive people.

AT THE LAKE, she strolled along the shoreline, thinking about the girls' growing up years. She and Dean had been so involved in their daughters' lives there wasn't much time for anything else. When Sarah went away to college, they realized things were changing. The girls were growing away from them.

Sarah's college was close, so it wasn't bad, but when Sami left, too, they felt the pains of letting go. Ironically, it was Dean who took it the hardest. Mainly, Claire supposed, because he'd never wanted to be like his father. He always wanted to be there for the girls. But now they didn't need him so much.

August, 2001

SAMI'S CAR WAS LOADED down with everything she thought she would need for college life. As she drove away, Claire and Dean stood in the driveway and waved until they couldn't see her anymore. Then he turned and went into the house.

Claire stayed where she was, feeling so many things she couldn't define. All she knew was that her babies were gone. Slowly, she made her way into the house. She looked for Dean, but couldn't find him. Then she realized exactly where he was.

In Sami's room.

She walked up the stairs and discovered him sitting on Sami's bed, holding one of her stuffed teddy bears.

Sinking down beside him, she wrapped an arm around his waist. "The house is quiet, isn't it?"

"Mmm." He nodded. "It seems like yesterday they were little girls chasing each other through the place. Where did the years go, Claire?"

"I don't know," she admitted. "When they were babies, the days were endless."

"Now we're older and looking back, and wishing we could recapture a moment of that time."

She kissed his cheek. "You're such a softie."

He laid the teddy bear on the bed. "I know I have a hard time letting go."

"You're a parent. You're allowed."

He glanced at Sami's trophies. "She played her heart out for those."

"She gave mine a workout, too."

"Yeah." He grinned and stood. "Just think, we have two daughters in college."

"And the tuition fees to prove it," she teased.

He looked into her eyes. "Yeah, and it's finally time for you to go, too."

She got to her feet and looped her arm through his. "I'm going three nights a week so I can keep my job at school."

"If you wanted to go full-time, I think we could swing it."

"We need my paycheck, because I want the girls to have the best educations. I'm happy with going part-time, and I have to be available Friday nights, to support my husband and his winning team."

"I love you."

She smiled. "That works out really well, because I'm head over heels in love with you."

They walked down the stairs arm in arm.

In the den Dean glanced around. "You know, we can watch TV in the nude if we want to."

She glanced at him. "Why would we want to?"

He worked an eyebrow up and down in a suggestive manner.

"Are you turning into a dirty old man?" Claire tried very hard not to laugh.

"Only with you, my love," he growled, and came toward her.

She shrieked and ran around the sofa. He came after her, and she zigzagged out of his reach a couple of times before he caught her.

He whirled her around and around. "Just you and me now."

"You and me," she echoed, and laid her head on his chest.

ON MONDAY DEAN DROVE to work with a heavy heart. As he turned onto Exposition Boulevard, he wondered what Claire was doing. He missed having morning coffee with her, but then, he missed everything about her.

She'd made so many sacrifices for their family. A deep guilt weighed him down. Somewhere in the last twenty-five years he should have found a way to make sure she got her degree. But family always came first.

When Sami left for college, they were both excited that Claire would go back to school. As before, though, life had a way of throwing up a roadblock.

January 2, 2002

CLAIRE AND DEAN spent the day taking down Christmas decorations. They'd spent New Year's Eve partying with the Mallorys and the Hudsons. Bunny had fixed New Year's Day dinner at her place and they had met the girls there. He and Claire talked about how quiet Bunny was. Usually she was chatty and cutting up with the girls. They put it down to the hustle and bustle of the holidays.

Dean stored the last box in the attic and was headed to the utility room for the vacuum when he saw his mom's Buick drive up. He hurried to the front door. The moment he saw her he knew something was wrong. Her blue eyes were filled with tears.

"Claire," he called, a moment before Bunny reached him. He had a feeling he was going to need his wife.

"Hey, Mom," he said, hugging her. As he did, he felt her tremble, and his heart ricocheted like a bullet off his ribs.

"Hi, Bunny." Claire came from the bedroom. "What a…" She paused as she noticed the tears. "What's wrong?"

Bunny wiped her eyes and didn't speak. Her complexion seemed to grow even paler.

Claire took her arm and led her into the kitchen. "Have a seat," she said, taking over the way she always did. "I'll make a pot of coffee."

Dean sat next to his mom, waiting for words he knew he didn't want to hear. Like a kid, he wanted to turn back the clock and stay in 2001. But the adult Dean braced himself.

Claire rushed back and put an arm around Bunny, rubbing her shoulder. "What is it?" she asked gently.

"I…I found a lump in my breast in December and…and I went to the doctor. He did a biopsy and I just got the results back. It's malignant and…I have to make all these decisions and I…I…"

Dean felt as if he'd been sucker punched, and anger shot through him. *Not his mother.* They'd been through hell with Sami, and then Robert's heart attack. They'd had more than their share. Not again.

And not his mother.

Claire hugged Bunny tightly and then knelt by her chair. "Dean and I are here to help you make those decisions— just like you were there for us. We are Rennelses and we're survivors. We'll beat this."

Bunny smiled through her tears. "I love you, sugar."

"I love you, too." Claire stood and hugged Bunny again. "What do you need us to do?"

"I have an appointment with the surgeon at ten in the morning. I'd like for you both to be there."

"We'll be there."

Dean stood on legs that wobbled like the time he'd had his lights knocked out in the Oklahoma game. "Mom…"

It was the only sound he could make. Bunny flew into his arms and he held her with arms that felt leaden.

"I'm sorry, champ," she mumbled. "You don't need this."

Dean looked at his mother—this incredibly strong woman who had gotten him through hell so many times.

"Hey, you're my mom and I love you. I'm going to be with you every step of the way. You can count on that."

"I'm scared," she whimpered in a broken voice.

Dean swallowed and fought for control. "Bunny Rennels, I never thought you were afraid of anything." He had to reach deep for the levity or else burst into tears.

She wiped at her eyes. "You're right. Cancer's not going to stop me."

But Dean wondered about that in the days that followed.

The next morning they sat in the doctor's office and listened to her options. The tumor was less than four centimeters, and the surgeon suggested a lumpectomy and lymph node removal, to be followed by radiation therapy.

They discussed mastectomy versus lumpectomy, and Bunny agreed with the latter. The surgery was scheduled for Friday.

The procedure went fine, and they were all there, including the Thorntons. Bunny was released the next day, and Claire and Dean took her home to Tarrytown. They'd fixed up the spare room, and Bunny was surprisingly happy with the situation. That told Dean how scared she was.

The girls hovered over the weekend, worried about their grandmother. Bunny was in pain and tried gallantly to hide it. Finally, he had to talk to Sarah and Sami and explain that Bunny needed rest. So they were all extra quiet. They took turns checking on her, but Claire seemed to be the only one Bunny wanted.

School was back in session and that presented a problem. Bunny had to have radiation therapy five days a week for seven weeks, and someone had to take her. He and Claire talked and they tried to think of a solution, but there really wasn't one. Bunny needed them, and Dean had learned early that there were things Claire could do that he couldn't, like help with dressing and bathing.

Claire once again dropped out of college, and spoke with her principal about taking a leave of absence from her teacher's aide job. Dean couldn't talk her out of it. He was hoping to pay someone to come in during the day, but Claire refused to let a stranger take care of Bunny. In truth, he felt better about the situation, but once again guilt was his constant companion.

The next seven weeks were a nightmare. The radiation burned Bunny's fair skin, and she was in so much pain. Then her arm and hand began to swell. The doctor was worried about infection, and she was hospitalized for a week. Once the infection was under control they adjusted the radiation therapy, and treatment started again.

Claire never left Bunny's side. She stayed with her in the hospital in case she needed anything. Claire didn't want her to be alone, and Dean loved his wife more than ever for her dedication to his mother.

But the radiation took its toll on Bunny. She became very tired and depressed and even the girls couldn't cheer her up. Strangely, the spark that got Bunny going again was Gwen. She visited many times, and one day she brought an old Monopoly game of Claire's.

Bunny had a hard time moving one arm, but no way was she going to let Gwen know that. She didn't want to appear weak in any way, or a burden to Claire and Dean. The game became a way of exercise for Bunny without her even knowing it. And she and Gwen formed a new friendship.

Bunny stayed with them a year before she finally decided she was going back to her place. The doctor said she was cancer free for now, and they were all jubilant. Dean's mom was eager to be on her own. But that first night was hard on them.

Dean slept restlessly, worried his mother might need something. He woke up to find Claire standing by the window.

"Honey." He pushed himself up in bed. "What are you doing?"

"Nothing." She shrugged. "I just wish Bunny didn't feel like she had to leave."

"She didn't. She wanted to have her independence back, and to give you *your* independence back."

"I know."

"Honey, she's healthy again, and walking and exercising, thanks to you. You've been wonderful with her." Bunny and Claire walked every morning. In the evenings, Dean walked with his mom, and on weekends the girls took turns exercising with their grandma.

Claire trailed back to the bed and crawled beneath the covers. "After all she's done for us, I could do no less, and I love her."

"Come here," he said, and she snuggled into his arms. "I love you and it's time to start thinking about college again."

She shook her head. "Not now. We have too many bills. I'm going to wait until Sami graduates and we've paid off some of our loans."

He held her a little tighter, knowing she spoke the truth, and hating that fact. With two daughters in college and a sorority, plus four vehicles, insurance and a house note, every dime he made was spoken for. Thank God the lake house had finally been paid off. But they had other expenses. His mom had health insurance, but it didn't cover much. He had to take out a loan to help pay off some medical bills.

"Honey—"

"Shh." She placed a finger over his lips. "Let's don't argue. Let's just be happy that we're all healthy."

Sometimes he wondered if that was enough. Robert had offered money, but Dean had refused. He hated how he let his pride get in the way, but he wanted to provide for his wife and his family. That was important to him.

Pride was very little comfort, though, when he looked back and saw everything Claire had given up. Sometimes he stopped believing in tomorrow and a better life.

But he never stopped believing in Claire and their love.

CLAIRE SAT ON THE PIER, trying to read a book. Ozzy darted out from the house next door followed by Mr. Weatherby.

She waved.

"Hello, Claire."

"Mr. Weatherby," she acknowledged. "It's a little warm today."

"I just wanted to check if the fishing line was still in the lake."

Sure enough, the red-and-white cork was out there, floating on the water. That was strange. When she'd sat down, she hadn't noticed it and thought the line had been removed.

"I'll call again. Someone is going to get hurt."

"Since the kids are back in school, there's not much activity," she said consolingly. "I'm sure they'll remove it as soon as they can."

"I'm still phoning."

Claire nodded, then frowned as a FedEx truck stopped at her house. A man got out with an envelope and strolled toward her. She immediately rose to her feet.

"Howdy, ma'am." He glanced down at the envelope. "I'm looking for Claire Rennels."

"I'm Claire Rennels," she replied, walking to meet him.

"Sign here, please." He handed her a wireless gadget with a pen and pointed to a line.

She put her book under her arm and scribbled her signature. As he gave her the envelope, he said, "Have a good day, ma'am."

"Thank you."

Going inside, she wondered why she was getting mail here. She ripped open the envelope and pulled out a letter. Sitting down, she began to read.

My sweet Claire,

I can't sleep without you here. That big bed is too lonely, so I'm camped out on the sofa, missing you, loving you.

You said we've lost that special connection. I've never felt that. We've been busy with our lives, but you're the light that guides me home. You're always in my heart and in my thoughts. We can get through this, honey. Please come home.

I love you.

Dean

She stared at the letter for a long time, his words reaching her in a way nothing else had. Laying it on the coffee table, she gazed out the window to the water gently lapping at the shoreline. He loved her. He understood.

Why wasn't that enough?

Their love had always been enough.

In that moment her heart broke, and tears oozed from her eyes. What was wrong with her? She was so confused, and struggling to make sense of everything she was feeling. But nothing made sense.

Except one thing.

She didn't want to be a mother at forty-three.

That truth curled through her stomach like the nausea she'd been feeling. And she hated herself and her selfish thoughts.

She brushed away tears and went for the ice cream. She needed something to cool her off.

DEAN SAT AT HIS DESK and wondered if Claire had gotten the letter. He kept waiting for the phone to ring, but every time it did it was school business.

His offensive coordinator, Eric Hudson, came in. "Hey, Dean. How's Claire?"

Dean tried not to squirm. They were good friends with the Mallorys and the Hudsons, and shared a lot, what with their kids growing up at the same time. But he didn't want to leak their unexpected news until Claire was ready. "A little better."

"Probably just nerves. You know how women are."

"Yeah." But Dean knew it was so much more.

"Justin wants to know if he's starting Friday night."

Dean studied the game plan in front of him. "What did you tell him?"

"That it's your decision."

"Do you think he's ready?" Dean already knew who was going to start, but he always asked for his coaches' input, and sometimes they changed his mind.

"He's ready, but…"

Dean leaned back. "But what?"

"You know his arrogance as well as I do. Sometimes that's a plus and sometimes it's a big minus. And then there are the girls. He's now dating Rachel Parson, and she's a big distraction for him. His focus is not one hundred percent on the game."

"And Russ Archer is more focused?"

Dean knew how Eric felt about Russ. The kid had personality plus and he was good, but he didn't have the arrogance and confidence of Justin. Of course, he was only a sophomore, and would grow into the role.

"You bet," Eric said. "But he doesn't have Justin's throwing arm. Another year, though, and college coaches will be taking a real good look at him."

"Yeah, but we're dealing with today and Friday night." Dean leaned forward. "Send Justin in."

"Sure thing."

Dean picked up another letter he'd written to Claire, and reread it. When his mother had suggested he needed to make his wife feel young and in love again, he'd thought of writing to her, just as she used to write to him. Claire knew he hated writing. Maybe this would show how sincere he was. Why hadn't she called?

"Hey, Coach," Justin said, plopping into a chair. "Why haven't you picked a quarterback yet? The first game is five days away and my dad said you should have done that by now."

Another minus for Justin. His dad, the ex-college-quarterback.

Dean looked up. "Your dad doesn't have any say in how I run my program."

"Uh, I know, but he's an expert at football."

"So am I, Justin."

The kid didn't have a comeback.

Dean never took his eyes off the boy. "Tell me why you deserve to start Friday night."

"Because I'm the best you've got."

"Russ is also good."

Justin's eyes seemed to dilate. "But he's a sophomore."

"I won't hold that against him."

The teen leaped to his feet. "You have to let me start. I'm the best. My dad said so and he's on the school board. He could get you fired."

Dean shrugged, always amazed at the kid's gigantic ego. "He's welcome to try. I coached junior high football until I was offered the head coaching job here ten years ago. I've never had a losing season, in junior high or here. I've taken the team to the playoffs six times. We won State twice. Everyone loves a winning team, and to fire a winning coach, well, like I said, your dad is welcome to try."

"But I'm better than Russ," the kid argued.

"Russ has a better attitude, he's a team player and he doesn't trip over his ego." And he didn't have a father who questioned a coach's judgment. But Dean wouldn't say anything about Justin's overzealous father. He would never cross that line.

Color drained from Justin's face and he swung toward the door. This was it. What the kid did now would determine the fate of the team this year. Part of Dean's job was to try and instill character and sportsmanship into these boys. He taught them about working hard and winning, and how, as long as they gave their all, there was no shame in losing. But sometimes boys like Justin tried his patience.

Until he curbed his arrogance and showed he could be a team player, Justin wasn't starting Friday night.

The teen stopped at the door and Dean held his breath.

"I told Rachel I was playing. Everyone expects me to start." The kid turned. His face was a sickly shade of gray.

Dean stared straight at him. "Do you want to begin this conversation over again?"

"Yes, sir." Justin hurried to stand in front of Dean's desk.

"What do you have to say?"

He swallowed. "I'm sorry for what I said."

Good. The kid had the right stuff, but outside influences were clouding his judgment.

"Thank you. I appreciate that." Dean picked up a pen and studied it. "Now, why do you want to start Friday night?"

Without even a pause, he responded, "Because I can win the game. I can be a team player, Coach."

Dean nodded. "Then you can start and Russ will be your backup."

"Thank you, Coach." Justin's eyes gleamed. "I won't let you down. I won't let the team down."

"That's all I ask."

The kid jogged out and Dean stared at the phone. Why wasn't Claire calling? He could reach seventeen-year-old boys, but he couldn't reach his wife.

Claire, please, just call.

CHAPTER FOURTEEN

CLAIRE SPENT THE DAY in a restless state of mind. She strolled along the shore, spoke to some neighbors she hadn't seen in a while—retirees without children at home. They were just enjoying the rest of the summer.

She walked until her legs grew tired and then she made her way back to the cottage. The McVees, her next-door neighbors on the far side, had a colorful red-and-yellow hummingbird feeder in their backyard under a gnarled oak tree. She stopped for a moment to watch the tiny birds feeding on the sugar water. Like dive-bombers, the small creatures flew in to propel their needlelike beaks into the slots in the feeder, hovering in space as they did.

Dozens of them swarmed around the bright feeder, fighting with each other to gain a spot at the trough, so to speak. They were magical in their intensity and amazing speed.

After a moment she walked on, the dry grass crunching beneath her sneakers. The sun was beginning to sink and a slight breeze stirred the tepid air.

She went inside and picked up Dean's letter.

She should call him.

But she wasn't ready. Besides, he was busy preparing for the first game of the season. She'd spent over half her life sharing football with him. It was a part of their very existence, but she wasn't sure she'd be in the stands on Friday night.

That shook her. She was always there to support Dean, to let him know she was behind him all the way.

She had no interest in going, though, and that shook her even more. She was just tired. Rest was what she needed most. Tomorrow she'd feel different. Tomorrow she'd come to grips with the fact she was a middle-aged pregnant woman doomed to repeating her mistakes.

Tomorrow was twenty-four hours away.

It seemed like a lifetime.

DEAN HAD DINNER with his mother. He'd given up on Claire calling. He realized the pregnancy was an agonizing situation for her, and he wanted to help, but he also realized she had to do this alone. He had to respect that. It wasn't easy, though.

Bunny placed a platter of pot roast, carrots, potatoes and gravy on the table. It looked delicious, but he didn't seem to have an appetite.

"When's Claire coming back?" she asked.

"She said by the end of the week." He wasn't so sure that was true.

"She'll be here." Bunny nodded, placing a glass of iced tea in front of him. "She won't miss the game on Friday."

Dean spooned food onto his plate, but he just toyed with it, unable to spark his appetite even with Bunny's hot buttered rolls.

He could feel his mom watching him.

"What's going on?" she finally asked.

He laid down his fork. "I'm worried, that's all. I want my wife back. I want our life back."

"Well, champ, this is where the rubber meets the road, isn't it?"

"I suppose."

Bunny broke open a roll. "Just put yourself in Claire's shoes."

"That's a little hard to do, Mom."

She thought for a minute. "I'm trying to think what my reaction would have been if I'd discovered I was pregnant in my forties and had a grown son."

"And?" he prompted.

"Slit my wrists comes to mind."

He was taken aback. "You would not."

She pointed her knife at him. "Let me tell you, champ, raising you alone wasn't a picnic. No way would I want to go through that again, and Claire's experiencing the same emotions."

"I know all that."

"Then just give her time and stop worrying." She took a bite of the roll. "Since the girls have grown up it's kind of lonely sometimes. This new baby is going to make us all young again, and I'm looking forward to it."

He gazed at his mother, who was always there for him through everything. Her sharp tongue and dry wit were just parts of her unique personality. And he realized he hadn't thanked her enough for all the things she'd done for him.

"Did I ever tell you how happy I am you stopped drinking and smoking?" he asked.

"Not really, but I knew you were."

"What made you stop?" He'd begged her so many times as a young boy to stop, but she wouldn't or couldn't.

Bunny shifted uncomfortably. "When Sarah was born,

I knew you weren't going to let me keep her if you thought I was drinking. And certainly not if you thought I was going to light up a cigarette. Claire was having such a rough time and she needed me. So I quit—cold turkey. I haven't had a drink or a smoke since. Claire and those girls gave me the best reason to stop."

Dean took a breath, knowing he had to say something else. "I'm grateful you decided to keep me after my father ran out on you."

Bunny had been a star basketball player in high school. She wanted to better her life away from an abusive family. She'd studied hard to get good grades and be eligible for a basketball scholarship. Her plans went awry when she met Douglas Rennels. Already out of school, Doug came to watch the games. Bunny was flattered by his interest and before long she was sleeping with him.

Dean had heard that history had a way of repeating itself, and in the Rennels family that was certainly true. Bunny became pregnant and lost her scholarship. Doug ran out on her, and Bunny's mother kicked her out of the house. Not for the first time Dean realized the enormous sacrifice she'd made for him.

Bunny looked up. "It wasn't a decision, champ. I just did it."

"But it had to have been hard. I know it was for Claire and me, and we were together."

"I just centered my life around you, and it was easy." Bunny placed her fork in her plate. "But I did need the liquor to face some of those days."

Dean reached for her hand, wanting to say something else. "Mom, I'm sorry I disappointed you by getting Claire pregnant in high school."

She squeezed his fingers. "You've never disappointed me. I've always been very proud of you. I just wanted to keep you from repeating my mistakes, but let me tell you something, champ. Claire and those girls were no mistake, and I'm so proud of the way you've stood by them. You're nothing like your father."

"It was important to me to never be like him."

Bunny looked toward the window, her eyes dreamy. "He wasn't all bad. He just had a hard time with responsibility." She took a deep breath. "I'm sorry I bad-mouthed him for so many years. I shouldn't have done that."

It was the first time his mother had ever admitted it, and in that moment Dean knew she was always going to love Douglas Rennels.

"You still care for him. Is that why you never had much of a social life?"

She glanced at him. "Maybe. But my mother had a string of boyfriends in and out of our lives, and I wasn't exposing you to that."

"Still…"

"Don't you worry." She winked. "I had a social life when you were over at friends, but no way was my kid having a stepdaddy. Then you started excelling in sports and I was right there with you."

"Yes, you were—always." He smiled at her.

"Like you and Claire were there for me. We're family, and that's what families do—help each other."

"We couldn't have made it through Sami's accident without you. Sarah depended on her grandma when her mother wasn't there."

"Even though she seems to be the Thorntons' favorite granddaughter, she and I have a special bond. And Sami's my little angel." Bunny took a swallow of tea. "Which reminds me, do Gwen and Robert know about the baby?"

"I don't think so. They're out of town, but I'm certain Sarah will tell them when they return."

"I wonder how they'll react."

"I'm not sure." He stood. "I've got to go."

"What? You haven't eaten a thing."

"I'm not very hungry."

"I didn't cook this for me, you know. I'll fix a plate for you to take home." Bunny hurried into the kitchen. "I have my cancer support group tomorrow night, the one Claire got me involved with. So you're on your own, champ."

"Mom, I don't need you cooking for me. I've been gone from home for a long time."

She handed him a foil-covered plate. "You'll always need your momma."

"You bet. I'll see you on Friday."

"Sarah and Sami are picking me up, and we're going to the game together. We're wearing our school T-shirts and we're prepared to scream our heads off."

He kissed her cheek and walked out the door. His mom and his daughters would be there.

But would Claire?

As HE OPENED his back door, Dean felt a sense of loneliness that was hard to describe. The house was empty and quiet. The TV or stereo was usually on and Claire was always buzzing around. She seemed to be in perpetual motion.

Tonight silence slammed into him, with more power than he'd ever felt, reminding him there wasn't much life without Claire.

Football didn't matter.

Nothing did, but her.

He was on the way to the refrigerator when the phone rang, and he quickly grabbed it, hoping it was his wife. But it wasn't. It was an old friend who was helping him scout for coaching jobs.

"Hey, Dean," Ralph Mullett said. "I got news. The California coach is definitely leaving at the end of the year. It's all top secret right now, but it's good to let the athletic director know you're available. So sharpen up that résumé, buddy. This is it. You know him and he knows your record of coaching winning seasons. This is a shoo-in for you. I have numbers, so get a pen and paper and be on the phone first thing in the morning."

This was where he made the crucial decision. What was more important to him—Claire or football? He took a deep breath.

"Dean, are you there?"

"Yes."

"Exciting, isn't it? They'll be interviewing a lot of people, but that's standard procedure. This is it for you, buddy."

"I'm sorry, Ralph, but I'm going to have to decline."

There was a long pause.

"Are you kidding me?"

"No. I'm quite serious. I need to be with my family."

"Oh. I hope nothing's wrong."

"Not really. I'm going to be a father again." He felt he owed Ralph a legitimate excuse.

There was another long pause.

"Damn, Dean, haven't you heard what causes that by now?"

"Thanks for thinking of me, Ralph. I appreciate it."

"No problem, buddy. I'll call in about a month and check on the status quo. You might change your mind. You have time."

"I won't."

As he hung up, he knew he wouldn't. This time he would be there for Claire completely. For the first time in days he felt at peace with himself.

And with the future.

THE NEXT MORNING Claire woke up with Dean's letter held tightly to her chest. She sat up and waited for the nausea. Nothing happened.

She made toast and an egg, and drank a glass of milk. Her stomach was fine. She showered and changed, feeling liberated. She strolled out to the deck and watched the beautiful morning awaken around her. The sun seemed to yawn and stretch as it played peekaboo with the gnarled oaks and cypresses, finally spilling unending sunlight across the water. Dust motes shimmered like tiny flecks of gold through the rays, catching every nuance of the morning light.

Spectacular. Beautiful.

There was nothing like the early morning.

A gentle wind was still blowing, and misty moisture touched her skin. She looked up to the blue sky, thinking rain might be in the forecast, but nothing showed in the clear, never-ending blue.

Out of the corner of her eyes she saw Mr. Weatherby and Ozzy strolling along the water's edge. He waved and Claire waved back. Her neighbor was checking the cork again. Evidently the lake personnel were busy and unable to take care of this small problem quickly enough to suit him.

Claire thought she might put on her suit today and swim

out and bring the cork and line to shore. That would give Mr. Weatherby some peace.

She'd started to get up when the FedEx agent rounded the corner.

"Mornin', ma'am," he said.

It was the same man so he knew who she was. He held out the gadget and she signed.

Handing her the envelope, he asked in a teasing tone, "Has this guy ever heard of a telephone?"

"It wouldn't be the same," she told him.

"Whatever," he mumbled, and strolled away.

She hurried inside. Her hand shook as she eagerly tore open the envelope. Sinking into a chair, she began to read.

My sweet Claire,
Remember Paris?
We made love in the shower, even though we had a comfortable bed. I finally know why we did that—to feel young again. We tried to recapture all those intense emotions we felt at eighteen. And we came damn close, didn't we? That time is forever imprinted in my heart.

As I think about the new baby, I know this child will make us young again. Even Bunny said so. This new life will empower us and make us strong and confident. We can do this, honey.

Come be young with me again.
Come home. I love you.
Dean

She drew up her knees, resting her chin on them. She remembered that time well. Dean was six foot four inches and she was five foot five. Making love in the shower with their height difference became a challenge.

An exquisite challenge.

She'd laughed and said the risqué scenario was for younger couples. That had only made them more determined. With their wet and slippery bodies braced against the shower wall, one of her legs tight around his hips, they'd more than accomplished it. They mastered it. There wasn't anything they couldn't do together.

Except deal with a pregnancy at their age.

She folded the letter and placed it by the other.

Come be young with me again.

His words kept running through her mind. She didn't feel young. She felt old and foolish. But his words were easing the resentment inside her. She could actually feel it, and she was elated. Dean always knew how to reach her. She clung to that hope.

THE DAY WORE ON and Claire stayed in with her thoughts. She planned to walk later when the heat wasn't so bad.

In the late afternoon she heard the sound of a car driving up to the house. She thought of the FedEx man and hurried toward the front door. When she heard the back door open, she swung around, and Sarah stood there.

Her eyes were red and her hair was disheveled. This was so unlike her eldest daughter that Claire's stomach clenched. Instinctively, she knew something was wrong.

Sarah flew into her arms and Claire held her tight. "What is it?" Claire asked into a tangled mass of blond hair.

Sarah drew back and brushed away tears with the back of her hand. "Nothing. I'm being silly."

Claire tucked her daughter's hair behind her ears. "Did you have an argument with Kip?"

She shook her head. "No. But I've decided to break up with him."

Claire took her arm and led her into the den. They got comfy on the sofa. "Do you want to tell me why? You were thinking about marriage."

"Sami was right. I don't love him." She flipped back her hair. "And I really hate it when she's right."

Claire knew that all too well. Sarah would fight with her last breath to prove Sami wrong. They were constantly trying to tell each other what to do. Claire supposed that was normal for two sisters so close in age.

"How do you know Sami's right?"

"I just do."

Claire watched the telltale red flush on her daughter's face. "Then why are you so upset?"

"Because…because…"

Claire took Sarah's limp hands in hers. "Sweetie, why are you so upset?"

"I don't love Kip the way you love Daddy."

Claire was taken aback for a moment. "What do your father and I have to do with your tears?"

"I told you it was silly."

"Tell me anyway."

"When Sami and I were growing up we always knew how much you and Daddy loved each other. You said it all the time, and you were constantly hugging, kissing and touching."

"You asked us not to kiss in front of your friends. You said it was embarrassing."

A tentative smile touched Sarah's lips. "Now that was really silly."

"Maybe. But it was the way you felt at that age."

"You and Dad are the best parents ever." Sarah's eyes sparkled with unshed tears. "And I want a love like that. I want a man who can't keep his hands off me, a man who will stick by me no matter what, and who will still love me if I'm forty-three and pregnant."

Claire felt a sense of trepidation. "Sarah, is this about the baby?"

"No, it's about your parents," she wailed. "How could they want you to abort me because they didn't approve of Daddy? How could they?"

CHAPTER FIFTEEN

CLAIRE'S TREPIDATION turned to fear. "Sarah, what are you talking about?"

"Grandpa and Gigi came back from Dallas today." Sarah gulped a breath and had trouble breathing.

"Where's your inhaler?" she asked.

"I…I don't…need it."

Claire hurried to her bedroom for her purse. Even though Sarah was grown, she still carried one for her.

When she handed it to her daughter, Sarah took several deep breaths. In a minute she was breathing better. Sarah rarely had spells, so the conversation with her grandparents must have been emotional. Sarah's triggers had always been emotional upsets, colds or flu and the weather.

After a moment, Claire asked, "What happened?"

"I went to tell them about the baby. They were shocked, but didn't say a lot. I had to get back to work, so I didn't stay long. I was in such a hurry I forgot my purse. When…I went back to get it, I heard them talking."

"What did you hear?" Claire asked in a quiet tone. They'd agreed to never tell the girls about the past. There was no need to. But now…

"Grandpa said it was just like before, and Gigi said they would let you make your own decisions. They wouldn't do anything so horrible as demand you get rid of the baby because they disapproved of Dean, like they had when you were pregnant with me. I…I must have made a sound or something, because they turned and saw me standing there. I ran to my car before they could stop me."

Sarah gulped another breath. "They…they wanted you to abort me because—"

Claire pulled her into her arms. "Baby, it was so long ago and I was their little girl. It had nothing to do with you. They didn't even know you. In their own way they were trying to protect me."

"I know. It was about Daddy. They didn't think Daddy was good enough for you, did they?" Sarah asked into Claire's neck.

Claire was struggling for answers, the right answers. But the right answers were entangled with the truth—a truth that would hurt her child. She chose her words carefully. "They didn't know him like I did, and they wanted what they thought was best for me."

Sarah drew back and wiped at her eyes. "I never questioned those years that they weren't in our lives. Suddenly they were there, our grandparents, and we loved them. But after hearing what I did… I can't understand how they could lose all contact with their only child because Daddy wasn't good enough to suit them. That makes me so angry."

Claire brushed Sarah's hair from her face. "Listen to me. I'm sorry you had to hear that. Try to think of how much your grandparents love you now. They truly regret what they put your father and me through. I've forgiven them and so has your dad. You can, too."

"I don't know," Sarah mumbled, her head bent. "I'm

always trying to please them. Sami tells me that all the time. And once again she's right. I'm becoming a lawyer because Grandpa wanted me to. I joined Gigi's sorority in college because she wanted me to. I started dating Kip because Gigi said he came from such a distinguished family, and I should think about what he could do for my future."

Claire was taken aback. She had no idea her mother had said that to Sarah, or tried to influence her. But Claire had only herself to blame. She was the one who had allowed her parents into their lives. She still had to believe it was for the best.

"But you wanted those things, too," she reminded her daughter. "You were excited about becoming a lawyer, you loved the sorority and you were quite taken with Kip."

"Yeah," Sarah mumbled again. "But I'm not sure I want it anymore. I feel different now."

Claire raised her daughter's chin. "Why? You're still my beautiful, intelligent girl. You have it all and the world is at your fingertips." She paused. "Just remember you have to live with the choices you make today."

An eerie feeling came over Claire—*just as she would have to live with her choice.*

Sarah curved against Claire's side as if she were five years old. "Tell me about you and Daddy and how you felt when you were pregnant with me."

"I was scared, so scared." Claire stroked her daughter's hair. "I was a teenager and going to have a baby, and I didn't know what I was going to do."

"What did you do?" Sarah whispered.

"I told your father and we decided to get married and become a family."

"Because you were in love?"

"Oh, definitely. Very much in love. And you and Sami are the symbols of our love. Every time I look at your shining faces I feel that love."

Just like the new baby will be another symbol of our love.

Claire was paralyzed for a second as a part of her opened up and accepted that reality.

That truth.

"Did you think about aborting me?" That tiny voice seemed to come from far away, but Claire heard it.

She collected herself. "The doctor said I had three choices—abortion, adoption or acceptance. Your father and I could only live with one of those choices."

"I love you, Mommy," Sarah whispered.

"Oh, baby." Claire hugged her. "Your father and I love you so much, and I really hate that you had to hear what you did today."

"I'm glad I did. I've been going out of my way to please my grandparents, and I suddenly realize I don't have to."

"No, you don't. But I also don't want you to do anything rash because you feel your father has been treated unfairly. Your dad and I fought that battle a long time ago and it's not your fight."

"Mmm." Sarah pushed her hair away from her face. "And you won."

"Yes, we did. And I'm sure if my parents had a second chance, they would do things differently. But we can't go back. We have to go forward. Because of circumstances, I became a strong, independent woman able to handle two babies, a household and a husband who had women throwing themselves at him."

Sarah grinned. "But Daddy only sees you."

"Yes," Claire replied, with the confidence a successful marriage had given her.

"You have a forever kind of love." Sarah's eyes grew dreamy. "That's what I want—a forever kind of love."

"Then don't settle for anything less."

"I won't." Sarah smoothed the fabric of her black slacks. "Would you do me a favor?"

Her daughter glanced up. "Anything."

"We've raised you to be a forgiving person, and I would like you to listen to what your grandparents have to say about the past. And I would like you to listen with an open heart." She touched Sarah's chest. "If you close your heart, all that resentment and bitterness will fester in you and you'll become hardened. I don't want that for you." Claire didn't want it for herself, either.

"How do I do that?" Sarah asked in that little girl's voice.

"Remember how much you love them and how much they love you. What happened in the past is exactly that— in the past. We all make mistakes. We're all human, with our own set of values and ideas. Sometimes we differ, but we learn to accept and forgive." Claire stopped for a moment. "Your grandparents adore you. They would never do anything to intentionally hurt you or Dean now. They respect your father a great deal."

Sarah fidgeted. "I guess I know that. It was just—" she blinked back a tear "—gut wrenching to hear."

"I've always been very proud of your strength and I know you can handle this like a discerning, loving woman."

Sarah shrugged. "Maybe. Maybe not."

Claire kissed her forehead. "I vote for maybe. And, sweetie, if you don't want to work in Daddy's firm, you don't have to. If you don't want to date Kip, you don't have to. Those are your choices. No one but yours."

"Yes." Sarah leaned back against the sofa. "When I heard Gigi say that, I couldn't get here fast enough. I'll be twenty-five in September, but I just wanted my mother to hold me and tell me she loved me. And that she loved my daddy."

"You know I do—always."

"Mmm."

They were quiet for a moment, and then Sarah asked into the silence, "Did you think about aborting this baby?"

Claire tried to swallow the enormous knot in her throat and failed. She thought she was choking, and had a hard time catching her breath. The truth weighed her down with a sick feeling. She wouldn't lie to Sarah, but exposing that truth would make her seem vulnerable, weak and selfish in her daughter's eyes.

She'd just told her about being human and making mistakes. Sarah was old enough to understand that.

"Yes." She finally swallowed. "I thought about it. But it wasn't an option, just as it wasn't twenty-five years ago."

Suddenly Sarah sat up straight. "I'll help, Mom. I really will. I know that sounds strange coming from self-centered Sarah, but I want to do this. I can move home and help at night and on weekends."

Claire felt such pride in her daughters and couldn't wait to tell Dean of the sacrifice they both were willing to make.

"Thank you, sweetie. I appreciate the offer, but the baby is your father's and my responsibility, not yours."

"But I want you to go to college like you planned. I was the reason you didn't go in the first place, and there's no reason for you not to go now. You'll have all of us to help."

"Let's get something straight. You are not the reason I didn't go to college. I was the one who chose to have sex with Dean. It was my choice and I have never regretted it."

"Then you are going?"

Again Claire had to be truthful. "I'm not sure yet."

"Mom, you know my mouth is always ahead of my brain. I'm sorry for what I said the other day."

"I know you are, sweetie."

"You're not too old to do anything. You can go to college, have a baby and run interference for two daughters, a lovable mother-in-law and two domineering parents. You can do it all. You are woman. Let me hear you roar." She sang the last part.

Claire laughed and they hugged. It all sounded good, but she still wasn't sure. Her daughter didn't need to know that, though.

The sound of a car drew them apart. Claire thought it was probably Sami. It wasn't. She felt Sarah stiffen as Gwen and Robert walked in.

"Why did you have to follow me?" Sarah got to her feet, defiance in every word.

Claire stood, too, and rubbed her daughter's arm, which seemed to help her relax. If Claire wanted peace and quiet, it definitely wasn't on her schedule today. The lake house had suddenly acquired a revolving door.

"Mom, Dad," she said, trying to figure out how to handle the situation. She suddenly wished Dean was here. He'd know what to say and do. But she'd just told Sarah how strong she'd become. Now she had to prove it.

Gwen came toward her. "Claire, darling, I'm so sorry this happened."

Claire didn't know if she was talking about the baby or

Sarah. Like her daughter, she tensed up, having no desire to go through this again with her parents.

"We didn't know Sarah was there. Robert and I were just talking about all the terrible mistakes we've made." Gwen looked at her granddaughter. "We never meant for you to hear that. We—"

"Why not?" Sarah asked point-blank. "You wanted Mommy to get rid of me because Daddy wasn't up to Thornton standards."

"Please, Sarah, don't talk like that," Gwen begged.

"How could you not like Daddy?" Sarah practically screamed the words. "He's honest, loving, kind and honorable. He's my father."

"We didn't know him," Gwen replied, her voice quivering. "We were only thinking about our daughter."

Sarah didn't respond, and Robert stepped forward. "I won't lie to you. We thought Dean was wrong for Claire." He cleared his throat. "We thought he'd taken advantage of her, and we desperately wanted to get her life back on track to accomplish all the dreams we'd talked about. But we never asked Claire what she wanted."

Sarah still didn't respond and Claire didn't intervene. They had to get all the good, the bad and the downright ugly out into the open now.

"In the end," Robert admitted, "we felt Claire chose Dean over us, and that hurt. It hurt our pride and damaged all the love we had for our daughter. But it wasn't long before we realized we'd made a terrible mistake. I sent Gwen with money, but Claire wouldn't take it. She was too proud."

Claire never knew her father had sent the money. She had thought it was all her mother's doing. She was learning things, too.

"I knew Claire's obstetrician and I asked him to call when Claire went into labor. Somehow Gwen and I needed to be there when you were born. We waited and waited for Dean to leave, but he didn't. He stayed in the hospital with Claire. I guess that's when I got my first glimpse of the kind of man he was."

"So you didn't see me?" Sarah asked, some of the defiance ebbing away.

"We didn't give up that easily," Robert replied. "We waited. They brought you back from nursing, and Dean stood at the window watching you for a long time. He finally went back to Claire, and we walked to the window before the nurse could close the curtains."

Claire was stupefied. "You were there? In the hospital?" She hadn't realized she'd spoken the words out loud until she heard her voice.

"Yes," her mother answered.

"Why didn't you come to see me?" She remembered the sadness she'd felt because her parents weren't there to witness her and Dean's wonderful miracle. And they'd been just down the hall. The thought was unbearable.

"Pride," her father answered. "Good old-fashioned pride. We thought we'd destroyed your love for us, and we weren't strong enough to handle the rejection if you refused to see us."

The sadness of it all tore through Claire. One kind, loving gesture from them would have meant avoiding a six-year stalemate. But she wasn't going to question that now. Life was exactly what it was—living through highs and lows and unbelievable irony. The only thing that concerned her at the moment was her daughter and helping her through this.

"But it didn't keep us from seeing our granddaughter,"

Robert added. "We thought you were the most beautiful thing we'd ever laid eyes on. You looked just like Claire. It was like looking at her baby photos. I had my camera so I quickly took a shot."

"You took a picture?" Again Claire couldn't manage to stay silent.

Robert reached into the back pocket of his trousers and pulled out his wallet. Opening it, he extracted a small photo. He walked over and showed it to Sarah.

Claire glanced at the worn photograph of her daughter, a little fuzzy from being taken though a window.

"I looked at this picture several times a day, as did Gwen. We didn't know how to correct our mistake until Sami's accident. Oh." He pulled out another photo. "I took one of Sami, too. These two little pictures were all we had for years."

This time Claire was speechless. They'd been there for both girls' births.

"Slowly, Claire allowed us back into her life," her dad continued, "and into Dean's and yours. I'll admit in the beginning we didn't think too much of Dean, but we've grown to love and respect him." Robert took a ragged breath. "I would rather die than hurt you, Sarah. Please believe that. I love you and Sami. You're the joy of our lives. I'm begging for your understanding and forgiveness, and this time I'm not letting pride stand in my way."

Sarah didn't move or speak, but Claire knew she had to let her do this on her own. As much as she wanted to nudge her, she couldn't. This was Sarah's decision.

"I'm so sorry you overheard us," Gwen interjected. "I never wanted you to find out how callous we'd been. And we were callous and unfeeling in our stance on Dean. Sometimes that's hard to admit. It seems like we are two different people now. Robert and I cannot even imagine a life without you in it. Such an existence wouldn't be worth living. We love you, Sarah, and I hope you've felt that love over the years."

Sarah nodded, hiccupped and then ran into her grandmother's outstretched arms, then her grandfather's.

Claire let out a long breath and wiped away a tear.

After a moment Sarah stepped back. "My father is the best man on earth."

"I couldn't agree more." Robert nodded.

"I'm not marrying Kip Willingham."

"Okay," Gwen replied calmly.

"And I'm thinking of finishing my internship in another firm."

Robert inclined his head. "That's entirely up to you."

Claire just stared at them. Were these her real parents?

"Are we having a party?" Sami asked from the doorway.

Claire had had an inkling her lovable worrywart would show up again today, and she was right.

Sarah hugged her grandparents again, kissed Claire and hurried toward Sami. Linking her arm through her sister's, she said, "I need a ride. We'll see you later."

"What?" Sami didn't budge. "Your car is outside and I haven't said hello to Grandpa and Gigi. Besides—" she held up a bag "—I brought Mom's dinner."

Sarah whispered something in Sami's ear. Her sister frowned, then walked over and hugged her grandparents, kissed Claire and handed her the bag. In a heartbeat the girls were gone.

Claire was left alone with her parents.

CHAPTER SIXTEEN

CLAIRE HURRIED INTO the kitchen and placed the bag in the refrigerator. Her legs felt wobbly when she was walking back to the den, so she sat on the sofa and braced herself for this conversation.

"Thank you for what you said to Sarah." She thought that was a good place to start.

"Oh, darling, please don't thank us." Gwen sat by her, placing her purse on the floor as Robert took Dean's chair. "We love Sarah and we were devastated she'd heard us talking."

"I believe Sarah was more hurt that you thought her father wasn't good enough."

"Claire, please believe we love Dean now."

"I know, and Sarah knows it, too. She's very protective of her dad. She adores him, as does Sami."

"I'm so sorry, but I'm very proud of you, darling. You've raised two strong, intelligent and compassionate women."

Her mother had said this before, but today it took on a whole new meaning. Claire felt a moment of pride and accomplishment. She was a mother. That's what she did best.

"And I meant what I said." Robert interrupted her thoughts. "Our lives would be so empty without you, Dean and the girls." He rubbed his hands together. "I often wish we had been more understanding and lenient with you in high school. If we had allowed you to date Dean, maybe your life would have been different."

He held a hand up as he realized what he'd said. "I really meant that maybe *our* lives would have been different. Maybe we would have been there for you like we should have been. And maybe our granddaughter wouldn't be feeling this pain today."

"Sarah will be fine," Claire told him, and she meant it.

"Why do you think they left so quickly?" Gwen asked.

"They're going to Dean." Claire knew that without any doubt. Sarah needed to see her father tonight, to let him know he was the best dad possible and that she loved him.

"Yes, of course." Her mom nodded. "The girls have a strong connection with their father."

"Yes, they do. As I said, they adore him. He always puts his kids first."

The same way he would with this new baby.

The baby.

Claire stood, feeling restless. "They left for another reason, too," she said. "They wanted to give us time to talk—in private."

"Why?" Gwen asked, seeming genuinely perplexed.

Claire took a deep breath. "Sarah said she told you about the baby."

"Yes," her mom replied. "Are you okay?"

"No," she admitted frankly. "I'm having a hard time dealing with the pregnancy." Claire held her breath as she waited for the speech about her age and about her rights and choices.

"Why?" her mother asked again.

"Is there something wrong, sweetheart?" Concern showed in her father's brown eyes.

This couldn't be her parents, she thought again. Had she really been afraid to tell them she was pregnant.

"I'm forty-three years old," she said, in case they'd forgotten that. "I have two grown daughters and I should be looking forward to a grandchild." She blew out a hard breath. "Instead I'm pregnant. I screwed up, and I know I've disappointed you once again."

"You haven't disappointed me." Gwen looked at Robert. "Has she disappointed you?"

"Not for a moment."

"Wait a minute." Claire ran both hands through her hair in frustration. "You're telling me you're happy about your middle-aged daughter having another child?"

"I'm ecstatic," Gwen replied.

What? Claire thought maybe she'd been out in the heat too long and it had somehow affected her hearing.

"You wanted me to get rid of Sarah, but you're okay with me keeping *this* baby?" The words came out before she could stop them.

Gwen stood. "Maybe it's because we demanded such a thing of you that we can now see how terribly wrong it was. And it's a second chance for us."

"What are you talking about?"

"We missed so much of the girls' early years because of our stubborn pride. We don't want to miss a second of this baby's life. In some small way it might make up for all the bad things we've done."

"We will help with the baby, too," her father said, his voice excited. "Babysitting free of charge anytime, day or night. Bunny's not the only one who offers those services."

Claire blinked back a tear. "Aren't you upset that once again I won't be going to college?"

Gwen shrugged. "That's up to you."

"Why can't you go?" Robert asked. It wasn't a criticism and he wasn't trying to pressure her. She could see he just wanted to know.

"Because I'm pregnant." The words sounded lame to her own ears, so she added, "And at my age there could be complications, or something could be wrong with the baby. Down syndrome is a real possibility."

"What's really bothering you?" Robert got to his feet. "You and Dean love each other. I know that hasn't changed even though you're out here by yourself. You've handled all of life's joys and disappointments together, and you'll handle this, too. So what's really bothering you, Claire?"

She flopped onto the sofa and drew up her knees. How did she open up and reveal a private part of herself? Some things were intimate, personal, secret. But she'd already told Dean. Now she had to say the words out loud, to admit the truth to her parents.

She took a deep breath. "I don't want to have another child."

"Oh, darling." Her mother sat down and put an arm around her. "That's understandable."

Her father sat on the other side of her. "Sure it is."

Their acceptance opened up that part of her she kept closed off from them. Dean knew her inner self well, but she had never exposed the real Claire to her parents. She wanted to be everything they wanted her to be, but sometimes that wasn't possible.

And sometimes a woman grew up and faced reality.

Her parents loved her. They would always love her. No matter what she did or revealed.

"I raised two wonderful daughters and I love them dearly, but I don't want to go through that again."

Her parents didn't say anything. They just let her talk.

"It's like starting over, and I don't want to start over. I want to go forward and enjoy these years with Dean. His dream job is coaching a college team, and I want him to have that. He's a great coach and he deserves it. But now he'll give up his dream and it's breaking my heart." She took a breath. "If he got a job offer out of town or the state, I planned to just go with him. I can attend college anywhere, and the girls are grown and on their own. We'd both realize our dreams. But now I've ruined everything by being careless and foolish."

"That's ridiculous, Claire," her father said, not trying to spare her. "A baby is transportable, you know, and can go anywhere you go."

"You don't understand." She rubbed her eyes in irritation.

"Then enlighten us," Gwen said.

"I gave everything I had to each of my daughters. I totally enmeshed myself into their lives and their welfare. At times I didn't know where I stopped and they began. I totally lost myself. There was never time for me, but that was okay. I was doing what I wanted—being a mother."

Her parents didn't speak so she went on. "I don't know if I have anything left to give this child. I don't know…" She buried her face on her knees and let the tears flow.

"Stop it, Claire," Gwen said, and stuffed a tissue in her hand.

She wiped away her tears. "I know…that's…selfish."

"It's human. That's all, so for heaven's sake allow yourself some leeway here. Stop beating yourself up for the way you're feeling."

Claire was spent and empty and had nothing to say.

"I remember another time you had dreams," her father told her. "And look how that turned out. Dreams sometimes don't unfold the way we plan. Sometimes they turn out better. I have two beautiful granddaughters because you fought for them, and I know you'll fight for this child, too." With one finger he reached for her wet chin and turned her face toward him. "Look deep inside you, because all those feelings are there, those feelings that guided you to make the right choices for your daughters, yourself and Dean."

She resisted the urge to bawl again.

"And we'll be there to help you all the way." Her mother handed her another tissue. "Your father and I need to help you this time, so please allow us to make this as easy as possible for you."

"And if Dean gets a job offer out of state, we'll follow," her father said.

Claire sat there, stunned.

"I'm sixty-seven years old and basically retired. I'll sell my interest in the firm and go wherever you and Dean go. You're all the family we have, and we're going to make sure we stay in your life this time."

"And if you want to go to college, I'll take care of the baby." Her mother joined in. "Either at home, or I'll go with you to class and wait in the hall, so you can nurse when you need to. I'll do whatever you want. We would like this baby to know who his or her grandparents are from the start. Please, Claire, let us help you."

She jumped to her feet. "Who are you? You can't be my

parents. If you were, you'd be berating me, telling me how foolish I am."

"Oh, darling." Gwen stood and embraced her. "This baby is a miracle who's going to bind us that much closer."

"Yes." Robert joined the embrace. "For Dean's sake I'm hoping it's a boy, but I'll love it no matter what it is, boy or girl."

A boy for Dean.

Standing in the circle of her parents' arms felt surreal, and Claire realized a lot of healing had happened tonight. But through all of the emotions, one thing stood out.

A boy for Dean.

AFTER HER PARENTS LEFT, Claire wanted to call Dean. She suddenly missed him terribly. But she knew the girls were there, and Sarah needed to talk to her father, to hear the story from his point of view.

What if her motherly instincts were wrong? She knew they weren't, though. For a reason that still wasn't clear to her, she didn't go home.

She walked out onto the deck, and found it was a clear, beautiful night. A full moon cast its beams toward earth, and Claire basked in the muted glow. She didn't even turn on the deck lights.

The warmth of the night enveloped her as she sat alone with her thoughts. A part of her soul had been bared tonight, and she knew the people who mattered most in her life loved her just the way she was, faults and all.

She hadn't accepted the pregnancy graciously, yet everyone seemed to understand. It was only she who found fault with her attitude and feelings. Claire wanted to be the perfect mother, and she had been for the girls. And now she knew the reason for that motivation. The abandonment of her parents had cut deep, and she'd strived hard not to be like them, giving up on their child.

There'd been no need to tell them that tonight. It would only hurt them, and they'd already seen how wrong they'd been. But through this realization something else became clear to Claire, the reason for her heartache over not wanting another child.

It made her more like her parents.

The child hadn't been conceived at a convenient time for her, and she was fighting against the intrusion of a life she hadn't planned. She was denying her own baby.

As her parents had denied her for so many years.

Oh God. A pain as sharp as an arrow shot though her heart. Tentatively, she placed her hand on her stomach.

The quiet and loneliness of the night wrapped around her. Crickets chirped and the hum of a motor could be heard on the lake. Familiar sounds, but she was feeling an unfamiliar pain.

Moving uneasily, she shifted her thoughts. She couldn't see the cork and she wondered if it was still there.

Something touched her ankle and she jumped completely into the chair, her heart in her throat. Ozzy looked up at her, wagging his tail.

"Ozzy, you little devil, you scared me half to death." She relaxed and eased her legs down, reaching to scoop the dog into her arms. "What are you doing here? Mr. Weatherby is probably worried about you."

She went down the steps and walked to her neighbor's back door. His deck was screened in but Claire didn't see him. She knocked and waited. There was no response so she knocked again and called his name.

She was starting to get worried when the door to the house finally opened and Mr. Weatherby stepped out. His silver hair was mussed and she knew he'd been sleeping.

"Claire, what…?"

"Ozzy was over at my place so I brought him home. I knew you'd be worried about him."

The older man scratched his head. "How did he get out?"

"I don't know." She handed over the small dog. "But evidently he's found a way."

"I'll put him in his crate tonight and tomorrow I'll check all the doors."

"Good idea. Night, Mr. Weatherby."

"Thank you, Claire."

She nodded and walked away.

Inside her house, she thought she should eat something. She checked out what Sami had brought. A salad. Perfect. Claire ate her fill and carried an Almond Joy candy bar to the couch. While eating the chocolate, coconut and almonds, she thought about how fruit would be healthier. Her shorts were already getting tight. Soon she'd be a blimp, just as she'd been with the girls.

She made a face, but didn't stop eating the candy.

Finishing it, she reached for Dean's letters and curled up in his chair, holding them to her chest and absorbing everything that was important to her.

DEAN HAD HAD A LONG DAY and he was tired. The game was two days away and he'd asked the coaches to drive the boys hard at practice, so they'd be ready for the pressure. Justin had settled down and it was helping the whole team.

Dean never liked to play mind games with the boys, and withholding the name of the quarterback position had been just that. Justin had expected it to be handed to him without question, however, Dean wanted him to learn the value of work, responsibility and team playing. The teen was in the habit of thinking he was a one-man show. That wasn't going to work on Dean's team.

He'd waited for a call or a visit from Justin, Sr., but so far the ex-quarterback was minding his own business. The last couple of days Justin was focused and becoming a team member. The other players looked to him for leadership, and that's what Dean wanted—for Justin to step into the role with character instead of arrogance.

The only problem now was the girls who hung around waiting for Justin, mainly Rachel Parson, a cheerleader. Dean couldn't fault the boy for that. Hell, he'd lost track of the number of times Claire had hung around waiting for him. No matter how many times he'd been thrown to the turf, once he saw her beautiful face all his aches and pains eased.

But now he couldn't ease her heartache.

And that hurt.

It hurt even more that she hadn't called. She had his letters, but still there was no response. The end of the week was getting closer and his mind was more on Claire than on football. What if she didn't come back? What if she couldn't accept the pregnancy?

He had to be prepared for those possibilities. But a part of him would never believe Claire couldn't accept another child. Never.

Claire, honey, please come home.

He got out of his car, though he dreaded going into the house. It was so lonely without her, and he was beginning to hate the sound of silence.

As he opened the door, he noticed the lights were on. Could—

Suddenly two beautiful blondes threw themselves at him.

CHAPTER SEVENTEEN

CLAIRE WOKE UP the next morning still in the chair, the letters clutched in her arms. Good grief, she'd slept in an awkward position and now had a crick in her neck. She stood and stretched her shoulders and spine.

She decided to soak in a hot bath. As she waited for the tub to fill, she also waited for the nausea to hit. But again it didn't. Maybe she was over the worst part.

Now there was a thought.

Or just wishful thinking.

She sprinkled the water with lavender-scented bath salts the girls had given her for her birthday a year ago. Sliding into the water, she sighed. It felt heavenly and the lavender lulled her into a peaceful state of mind.

After thirty minutes she got out and dried herself. Her hand stilled over her slightly swelling stomach. Of course, that might not be all baby. Middle-age spread came to mind. She knew her hips and butt were bigger than they used to be, and with the baby they were going to expand even more.

She considered that cruel and inhuman punishment for a woman her age. At eighteen she hadn't worried about the weight. As she slipped into a pair of shorts, she decided she wasn't going to worry about it now, either.

Marching into the kitchen, she made another decision.

From this moment forward she was going to be upbeat and positive about the baby. She had to for her own peace of mind.

After breakfast she suddenly wanted to talk to Bunny. Claire missed her and knew she wouldn't call. She was a rare mother-in-law who actually respected other people's wishes. And Dean would have told her Claire wanted some time alone.

Bunny answered on the second ring.

"Bunny, it's me."

"Hey there, sugar. How are you doing?"

"Okay, but I found out something about myself."

"What's that?"

"I don't like quiet."

"With two daughters and a man who always has some kind of sports on the TV, I'm not surprised."

Claire smiled, able to visualize Bunny in her mind. She was sitting at the kitchen table reading the paper and drinking coffee. She was in her bathrobe and hair curlers, since she refused to use a curling iron. How she slept in the rollers Claire never knew. It seemed they'd be painful.

"Sarah and Sami came by last night," Bunny was saying.

Claire sat up straighter. "How's Sarah?"

"Sugar, she's fine, so stop worrying. She was just indignant about the way the Thorntons treated Dean. I told her that's all in the past and we're not dredging up old heartaches. She went to talk to her daddy, and I'm sure Dean soothed her wounded pride."

Claire knew she'd go to him. He had a way with kids, especially his own.

"After they left, Gwen and Robert stopped by for a visit."

"They did?" This really surprised her, but since

Bunny's cancer scare her mother-in-law and her parents had struck up a strong friendship. Jealousy wasn't such an issue anymore.

"Yes, and we had a nice chat."

"We had a good talk, too," Claire said.

"We're ready for babysitting duties. You just have to say the word."

Claire bit her lip and was silent for a moment.

"Sugar, are you there?"

"Bunny, I'm afraid I can't give this baby what I gave the girls. I don't know if I have anything left. I feel like I'm abandoning my baby, like my parents abandoned me. I… I…" It was easy to talk to Bunny.

"What, sugar?"

"I feel like I won't love this baby." She finally said the words that were causing all her pain. She'd skirted around them so many times, used other excuses. But now she knew.

And so did Bunny.

"What are you talking about? 'Abandoning'? 'Not love'? Never in this lifetime. The Claire Rennels I know has so much love in her she absolutely glows with it. You're stronger and more mature now, and this baby will feel all that experience and love. Your hormones must be spiked with gin or something, sugar, to have you talking like that. Because you don't have to worry about such a thing."

"You don't think so."

"I know so. I went through this with you and Dean the first time, and I don't know of another woman on this planet who could handle motherhood any better. And you babied a mother-in-law for a solid year. Not many women would put their dream aside to do that. Let me tell you, I know the real Claire Rennels, and she's the cornerstone of this family. So you're having a hard time adjusting to the pregnancy. So what? Any normal woman would."

Bunny always knew what to say to make her feel better. "I love you, Bunny."

"I love you, too, sugar. I just want you to come home and put my boy out of his misery."

"I'll be home soon."

"I never interfere. That's my motto, and I've lived by it all these years."

"It's one of the things I love most about you."

"Well, I'm fixing to break my motto because I feel you need to know this. Dean got the call about the California job he was expecting, and he said he wasn't interested."

Claire rose to her feet. "Bunny, no."

"He did. That's how committed he is to you and the baby."

"I didn't want him to do that."

"Remember what you tell the girls—sometimes you have to make choices you can live with. Well, that was the only choice for him. You've been his whole world since third grade and, sugar, nothing is ever going to change that."

"Oh, Bunny. I said some awful things to him and I didn't mean them."

"Spiked hormones, hmm?"

"Something like that. I want Dean to have his dream."

"He wants you to have yours, too."

"I know." Claire paced back and forth.

"It's time for you to talk to Dean."

"Yes," she admitted. "I love you."

"Love you always, sugarplum."

Claire replaced the receiver and strolled outside to the pier. She watched the gentle lapping of the water. The heat of the sun bore down on her and she felt its warmth radiate through her. Everything she'd thought and relived over the past few days held her spellbound. One thing made itself very clear.

She wanted to go home and sleep in her husband's arms.

Turning, she noticed the cork. Before she left, she'd remove the fishing line for Mr. Weatherby.

As she headed to the house for her swimsuit, she saw the FedEx man. *A letter from Dean.* She broke into a run, her heart hammering against her ribs.

"Good morning," she said, even though it was almost noon.

"I see you're expecting this one." The man smiled and held out the wireless device.

"Yes," she replied, signing her name. "This will be the last one. I'm going home today."

"Good for you." He handed her the envelope. "I wish you all the best, ma'am."

"Thank you." She waved and ran into the house, ripping open the cardboard. Sinking into Dean's chair, she began to read.

My sweet Claire,

Last night our beautiful daughters were waiting for me when I got home. I knew there had to be a reason, but it sure wasn't what I was expecting.

Sarah mostly wanted to talk, and we did for over two hours. They ordered pizza and had rented a couple of movies—*The Longest Yard* and *Friday Night Lights.* Are our daughters wonderful, or what?

I explained the past to Sarah, using Cam as an example. Parents are very protective of their children, and you were Robert and Gwen's only concern. I told her we'd gotten beyond the heartache and now she had to.

She's planning to make some changes in her life, so be prepared for that.

The girls spent the night and slept in their old rooms and it had me thinking about a space for the baby. I don't think I can redo their rooms. At least not yet. I want them to always have a place in our home. I can almost see you frowning. I know I have a hard time letting go, but life can be rough sometimes, and I want our girls to never be afraid to come home.

I thought we'd make the spare bedroom downstairs, the one we had planned for Bunny, into a nursery. I even went by Lowe's and looked at colors but you know I'm hopeless at that.

This letter is rambling on, but as long as I keep writing I can feel you're here with me. I have to go, though. I have to make it to the FedEx office and get to school. Today is the big talk. I'll tell the players about winning and losing and about sportsmanship. I'll tell them they can win the game tomorrow, but they have to want it. Not me. Them. Then I'll ask them how badly they want it.

And this is where I get the blank, puzzled or confident stares. I'm hoping it's all confidence today, because this team is good. I just have to coach them in the right direction.

Today I find I'm asking myself the same thing—how badly do I want it? And I'm not talking about the game. I'm taking about our life. If you're not happy and smiling, then my dream means nothing. I don't want it that badly. I only want you.

Come home, honey.
I love you.
Dean

Claire sat for a long time just savoring his words. "I'm coming home," she said. In that moment she knew they were going to make it. With this much love, how could they not?

They still had the future to sort out, but she was confident they could do it now. All those motherly feelings she yearned for would fall into place.

Within minutes she had her carryall packed. She noticed the letters on the coffee table and went back into the bedroom. Digging in a drawer, she found what she wanted—a ribbon. A baby-blue ribbon. Was that significant? she wondered.

She folded Dean's letters neatly, tied them together with the ribbon and placed them with her old love letters. As she straightened something on the lake caught her eye. She walked to the windows and saw something floundering in the water.

What in the world?

It took her a moment to figure out what it was. The splashing was in the area of the cork. Then it came to her. Ozzy! He was caught in the fishing line. He must have tried to reach the Hilmans' again.

She yanked open the door and ran outside, shouting for Mr. Weatherby. There was no activity at his house and she didn't have time to roust him out. Ozzy didn't have time, either.

Kicking off her sneakers, she waded into the warm water and then swam toward the terrier.

"Hold on, Ozzy, I'm coming." She thought if he heard her voice he wouldn't be so terrified.

Reaching him, she grabbed his wet, struggling body. "It's okay, Ozzy." The dog was completely entangled in the fishing line and she wasn't sure how he was staying afloat. He was trembling severely, but now she had him.

"It's okay, Ozzy." She tried to soothe him again. Now she had to untangle him, but the line was too tight. She treaded water, keeping them afloat and trying to figure out what to do. As she investigated further, she realized the line was tight for a reason. There was something on the other end.

The whole line had come unwound from the reel and the cork had shimmied to the end. It was held in place by the rod and reel on the bottom; the rest of the line was un-raveled in the water. She used her free hand to tug on it. It gave for a second and then she felt something around her ankles. The line. And there had to be a fish on the end of it. A big fish. That's why she'd seen the cork at times and other times hadn't. When the fish swam away, the cork went under.

She kicked out and then realized her mistake. The fish swam around her legs and the long expanse of line went with him, wrapping around one ankle.

Oh, no! She kicked out again and the fish swam away. The motion took her and Ozzy down, under the water. Panic seized her and her lungs were tight as she flailed her free arm and leg, trying to reach the surface.

She couldn't breathe. She had to have air.

Ozzy! The dog was probably getting water in his lungs. *OhmyGod!*

To save them, she jerked the line with her foot, and used

her other leg and arm to surge to the surface. Gasping for air, she screamed for help, but there was no one to hear. Mr. Weatherby was probably sleeping. The McVees were gone and the Hilmans must be, too. The cove was deserted.

Ozzy was limp now, unmoving, but she wouldn't let him go.

Fear filled her chest as she struggled in the water—struggled to stay alive.

"Dean," she screamed as the fish jerked her and Ozzy underwater one more time. Submerged in the lake, she fought with everything in her. It seemed like a useless battle. She was caught in a watery trap.

She was going to die.

My baby!

That one thought gave Claire the added strength she needed. She jerked her foot with all the strength she had, and felt the line cutting into her skin. But it yielded and she surged to the surface, gasping for every precious breath.

She coughed up some water, glanced at the sky and prayed. "Please save my baby. Please."

With Ozzy in one arm, she tried to stay afloat, but her strength was waning. She felt the tug once again and screamed, "Dean," as the line pulled her under.

DEAN HAD A FEW MINUTES before the players gathered in the gym. Most coaches had the big talk the day of the game. He would give one tomorrow, too, but he'd learned a long time ago that players were so keyed up before a game they never listened closely. Today he had their full attention. This method worked well for him.

But today he was distracted. He glanced at the picture

of Claire and the girls on his desk. Suddenly an eerie feeling came over him. It was ludicrous, but he heard Claire calling him. The hair rose on the back of his neck.

He jumped to his feet, not knowing what he intended to do. Robert walked through the door and noticed his strange expression.

"Dean, what's wrong?"

"I don't know." He shook his head. "I feel as if Claire needs me."

"She does. She needs you more than anyone."

Dean sank into his chair, worried now in a way he hadn't been before. Was something wrong? Claire would call if there was, he told himself.

He drew a deep breath. "Is there a reason you stopped by, Robert?"

"Yes." He took a chair across from Dean. "I just wanted to touch base with you about Sarah, and apologize for it ever happening. Gwen and I are so sorry, Dean."

"I didn't want her to find out like that. Hell, I never wanted her to know."

"We didn't, either, but she forgave us."

"That's my girl. Just like her mother."

"She sure is."

Dean stood. "Try not to worry. Claire and I will make sure she's okay."

Robert got to his feet also. "I always thought no man would be good enough for my daughter, but I was wrong. You're more than good enough, and you have exceeded this father's expectations."

"Coach, we're ready," Eric shouted from the hall.

Dean walked around his desk and hugged Robert. "Thank you."

Dean had waited years to hear those words, and they came at a time when it didn't seem to matter anymore. He knew it would when he had time to reflect. Right now he was just worried about Claire.

As he walked away, that eerie feeling followed him. After the meeting, he had to talk to his wife.

CHAPTER EIGHTEEN

CLAIRE FOUGHT HER way to the surface one more time, still holding on to Ozzy. She didn't know how much longer she could keep it up. But she was fighting not only for herself and Ozzy, she was fighting for her unborn child.

As she tried to stay afloat, the water lapping at her face, she forced herself to think. They were staying in one spot, the same place the cork had been all week. That meant something was anchoring the fish here. The rod had to be hung on something on the lake bottom.

Every breath was a gasp, and her legs were getting so weak. She couldn't even feel the line wrapped around her ankle anymore. Ozzy was limp in her arm. She didn't know if he was dead or alive. She had to do something and she had to do it now.

But what? *Think,* she kept repeating to herself. She needed both hands; she knew that for sure. Ozzy was tangled in the line, so he wouldn't go far.

"Ozzy, I'm going to let you go for a minute." She released her grip and he splashed with his legs to stay afloat. He was alive.

Claire had to act quickly. She drew a strong breath and dived under, grabbing the line with both hands and jerking it with all her might. The fish wiggled and pulled away from her, tugging on her leg.

A moment of helplessness gripped her. She wouldn't give up, though. Her baby depended on her. Once again she yanked, so hard she thought her arms would come out of their sockets.

Then, just like that, something snapped and released. She kicked her foot free and rose to the surface, spitting out water with a gasp. Then she reached for Ozzy, trying to untangle him. But he was trapped like a sausage in a casing.

She worked frantically with the line, but there was just so much of it. Without the weight of the fish, the strand around her ankle floated away, and she was finally able to work Ozzy free. She swam for shore and collapsed onto the bank, totally spent. The terrier lay limp and unmoving beside her.

Flipping over, Claire dragged in a breath of fresh, life-giving air. She stared up at the bright blue sky and whispered, "Thank you," as she rested her hand on her stomach. They say all things happen for a reason, and as she sucked in each delicious breath she recognized how true that was. The moment the baby was at risk she'd realized how important it was to her, how much she loved it and how much she would fight to save it.

Always!

Closing her eyes, she let the truth of that run through her.

She was a mother.

Always a mother.

"Claire, Claire. Oh good heavens, Claire!"

She opened her eyes to see Mr. Weatherby running

toward her. She managed to push herself into a sitting position and place a hand on Ozzy. He was breathing, but every bit as exhausted as she was.

Mr. Weatherby fell down beside them, his own breathing labored as he scooped his pet into his arms. "What happened?"

Claire wiped lake water and mud from her face and told him about the fishing line.

"I was looking for Ozzy and saw you swimming toward the bank, and I knew it had to be something with that damn cork. Someone's going to get an earful. You and Ozzy could have drowned." He stroked the dog and Ozzy whimpered.

Mr. Weatherby glanced at her. "Are you okay?"

"I'm going to be fine." For the first time she really believed that. For the first time she knew it without any doubts, resentment or ambiguity.

Suddenly all the anger she'd felt in the past few days disappeared. It was replaced with a burning desire for motherhood.

And for the future.

With Dean.

"What you did was very dangerous, but I appreciate it." He nuzzled the wet terrier and Ozzy licked his cheek. "My wayward dog appreciates it, too. Thank you."

Claire managed to stand. Water dripped from her and mud caked her skin. But she was alive. Her baby was alive. And she was deliriously happy.

Her legs trembled from fatigue and she would have crumpled to the ground if Mr. Weatherby hadn't caught her. She wasn't even aware he'd gotten to his feet.

"I don't believe you're fine, Claire. I'm going to call Dean."

"No. I'll call him." She wanted to do that herself, so he'd know she was okay. "I'm fine, really." She took a long breath. "I'm going to have a baby."

"What? You must have hit your head."

"No, I haven't," she assured him. "I'm really going to have a baby."

"Well, then, we need to get you to a doctor."

She could see he didn't believe her. He was only trying to pacify her.

"All I need is my husband, and I'm going home to him." She reached up and hugged Mr. Weatherby, uncaring that she got mud on his pristine pin-striped shirt. "Take care of Ozzy."

She walked toward her house, feeling stronger. Stripping out of her wet, muddy clothes, she took a shower and washed away the trauma of the day. She grabbed a towel and wrapped it around her. She found antibiotic ointment in the medicine cabinet and applied it to the cut the fishing line had made on her ankle. Her hands were also red from pulling on the line.

Suddenly an overwhelming weakness assailed her, and she sank to the tiles. A hysterical bubble of laughter escaped her. She was spending a lot of time on the bathroom floor these days.

Drawing up her knees, she rested her forehead on them. Suddenly the laughter turned to sobs. Heartbreaking sobs racked her body and she let them flow freely. She couldn't stop them even if she'd wanted to.

For the first time she accepted the child inside her and knew she would love it beyond measure. Why she'd ever doubted it, she wasn't sure. Maybe her hormones *were* spiked with gin.

She and Dean were having a baby.

And that sounded just like it should—wonderful.

She raised her head and tears fell onto her stomach. Placing both hands gently on the swelling mound, she said, "I'm sorry, little one. I'm so sorry your mother had a major meltdown. I love you. Please know I will always love you. Your daddy loves you, too. Your sisters and grandparents are going to spoil you so rotten. Your life will be filled with love. I promise you that."

Pushing against the floor, she rose to her feet, one hand still on her stomach. "Now we have to go home and see your daddy. I can't wait to see him. How about you?"

She had talked to the girls constantly while she was pregnant, and she was going to do the same with this baby. She couldn't seem to stop once she started.

Gathering the dirty clothes, she shoved them into a plastic bag and quickly dressed. She paused as she saw the backpack from the girls on her dresser. Slipping her arms through the straps, she adjusted it on her shoulders.

"How do you feel about college, little one? Your mother has had this dream for a very long time, and she's thinking about doing it all. I just single-handedly saved our lives. Surely I can handle college and a baby." She hummed as she picked up her bags and headed for the den. "I am woman. Hear me roar. Your sister put that thought in my head and I'm thinking she's right."

In the den she saw the letters and picked them up. Holding them to her heart, she felt the love that had saved her and guided her home. She placed them in her purse and headed for the door, smiling.

DEAN WAS HALFWAY THROUGH the speech when Eric came up to him. "You have an emergency call. I'll take over."

Dean didn't question him. The eeriness he'd felt earlier intensified and he knew something was wrong.

His blood ran cold as he listened to Mr. Weatherby. "She wasn't making a lot of sense and I think she hit her head on something. After I bathed Ozzy I went over to check on her, and I saw her car leaving. I thought you should know."

"Thank you, Mr. Weatherby. I'll take care of it." Dean stood for a moment, totally paralyzed. She must have been in the water fighting for her life when he heard her today. When he thought how close he'd come to losing her, a shuddering chill ran through him.

"Coach? Dean?" He heard Eric's voice, but it took him a moment to respond.

"I've got to go home. Take over for me."

"Sure. Is—"

But Dean didn't hear the rest of the sentence. He was running to his car. Seconds later, he was pulling out of the parking lot. He knew he was speeding, but he didn't care. Getting home as fast as he could was his main concern. When he turned into their driveway, he didn't see her car, and it wasn't in the carport at the back of the house.

Damn it!

He backed out and headed for the lake. Maybe she'd had engine trouble, or blacked out from the head injury Mr. Weatherby thought she had. Dean kept his eyes glued to the highway, looking for her car.

Nothing.

He couldn't let himself think. He just had to find her.

When he turned into their driveway at the lake, her car wasn't there. Lake personnel in a boat were, though, and they were removing the fishing line from the water. Mr. Weatherby was watching them, Ozzy at his feet.

Dean jumped out of his car and ran to his neighbor. "Has Claire been back?"

The old man turned, shading his eyes from the sun. "No, I haven't seen her since she left, about two hours ago."

"Thanks. I'll talk to you later."

Dean crawled back into his car and headed for home again. Maybe he'd missed her. She'd been gone two hours, though. That meant she went somewhere else first. But where?

His nerves were tight and stretched to the point where he couldn't think straight. He just wanted to see his wife's face, to know she was okay.

The drive seemed to take forever. Soon he turned off the MoPac Expressway and headed for Tarrytown. As he whipped into the driveway, he saw her car and sighed with relief.

Thank God!

He killed the engine and was out of the car in a split second. As he ran toward the back door, he searched his pocket for his house key. His fingers were stiff and shaking. Luckily, when he turned the knob, the door opened. It wasn't locked.

He hurried inside and stopped short in the den. "Moon River," one of Claire's favorite songs, was playing on the stereo, and she was dancing around the room. She had on the backpack and a baby rattle tucked behind one ear.

And nothing else.

Her blond hair cascaded around her shoulders and her naked body swayed enticingly to the music. She looked as beautiful as ever. Her breasts were fuller, as were her hips, but she would always be eighteen to him.

The worry inside him eased and was quickly replaced with a warmth he knew well.

Claire swung around and saw him. She smiled, and he knew in that instant his wife was back.

She held up her arms. "What do you think, Coach? Is this appropriate for college?"

He raised an eyebrow. "Probably not. But it works for me."

She slipped off the backpack and stretched out her hand. "Would you like to dance?"

"Most definitely." He walked forward and took her into his arms, and they floated around the room. She was tantalizing, seductive. She was everything she'd always been to him.

His woman.

His wife.

She lifted her head from his chest and his lips met hers in a sealing, forever kind of kiss. She wrapped her arms around his neck and he locked his arms around her, needing to feel every naked inch of her. They held nothing back, both taking and giving until they collapsed onto the sofa.

She reached up and gently stroked the hair from his forehead. "We're having a baby."

"Yes. I heard." He pulled her onto his lap and removed the baby rattle from behind her ear. "I've been so worried."

She nestled against him. "I'm so sorry I said all those awful things, especially about the vasectomy."

"I should have had it done long ago."

She kissed his neck. "Then we wouldn't be having this baby."

"No."

"Ask me that question again."

He didn't have to ask what question. He knew. "I believe we can be very good parents at our age, do you?"

"Oh yes, I now believe." She gazed at him. "Thinking about our full life together got me through, and your incredibly sweet letters guided me home. I could feel all that love again, and I had to, because I was so afraid I would resent the baby and wouldn't love it."

"Oh, Claire."

"I had too much gin or something."

"What?"

"Never mind. I said that wrong. Bunny said—"

"You don't have to explain. If Mom said it, I wouldn't understand it, anyway." He gently tucked her hair behind her ear. "Mr. Weatherby called, and I've been worried sick."

Claire sat up. "I told him not to do that."

"He was just worried. Tell me what happened?"

She told him about the nightmare in the water.

"Oh my God, Claire." Dean tightened his arms around her. "I knew you were in trouble. I felt it. Please don't do anything like that again." He looked into her eyes. "Are you okay?"

She touched the tip of his nose. "I'm better than ever. I want this baby now. I want it with all my heart."

"And college?"

"I'll be in class Monday morning. I'm a woman and I can do it all, or at least that's what Sarah tells me. And so did you."

"Yes, and I'll be right here to help."

Her fingers played with a button on his shirt. "Call the California people and tell them you're interested."

"No, honey. That job isn't for me. For now, I'm happy right where I am—with you, the baby and the girls."

"Dean…"

He locked his arms around her. "Let's not argue about it. Something else will come along and maybe I'll be ready then."

"Okay, for now."

He stroked her arm. "I came home earlier and you weren't here. Where were you?"

"I got to thinking about the ordeal in the water, and I wanted to make sure the baby was okay, so I went to see Dr. Carter."

"And?"

"He said everything seemed fine. My blood pressure was a little elevated, but he said it could be from the trauma. I have an appointment next week for a thorough checkup." She raised her foot. "I'm probably going to have a scar, though, from that stupid line. A little reminder of how precious life is."

He kissed the welt on her ankle. "You're precious to me."

She rested her face in the crook of his neck and he breathed in the sweet scent of her skin. "I love you," he whispered.

"Ah." She sighed. "I love you, too, and I love the way you smell."

"How's that?"

"Tangy and masculine, and tonight I want to sleep in your arms until the morning light."

He kissed the top of her head. "That can be arranged, and may we never have to sleep apart again."

"Amen." She tilted her head back, her eyes bright. "We're having a baby. Are you ready?"

"You bet, honey. I'm ready for the next twenty-five years."

"Me, too."

He kissed her gently, softly, reverently, and knew their

love had survived and would continue to do so. Because above everything they loved each other.

He swung her up in his arms and headed for the bedroom.

EPILOGUE

May, Four Years Later

CLAIRE GRADUATED summa cum laude and walked across the stage to receive her Bachelor of Science degree in education. As she shook the dean's hand, she heard a tiny voice in the audience.

"Mommy, can you see me?"

She could see her three-year-old son, Robert Dean, clearly. With his big blue eyes and dark hair, he was a replica of Dean. He sat on his daddy's shoulders, waving his hand to get his mommy's attention.

She blew him a kiss and he caught it and held it to his tiny chest. This little boy was the light of their lives. He made them younger every day, and Claire couldn't imagine a life without him in it.

Her whole family was here—Sarah on Dean's left, Sami on his right, with grandparents flanking them. As she stared at them she realized her father was right. Sometimes plans don't turn out the way we think they will. They turn out better.

Dean's team had won the state championship four seasons ago and he'd received a job offer as head coach at a small college forty-five minutes from their home.

He'd turned that team around in two years. When they beat a top-ranked school on national television, the offers came pouring in, including one he wasn't expecting—from a team in the NFL. He was now an assistant coach in Dallas.

They'd bought a house there and moved in. Come fall Claire would be teaching third grade in the school their son would attend. Bunny lived in a retirement villa a mile from them. Sarah was working at a law firm in Dallas, and Gwen and Robert had also moved to the city. Sami was the only one left in Austin. Claire and Dean worried about her being alone, but she loved her job, and they gave her the freedom to make choices without weighing her down with guilt. They kept the house in Austin because it was their home and they might return one day.

Claire waved at her family now, her beloved family. Whatever she did in life would never match her role as a mother.

After the birth of their son, the truth of that became even clearer. She took a year off from college to be with him, to give him her undivided attention, just as she had given the girls—not because she felt she had to, but because she wanted to. When he was through nursing, she went back full-time. Her children had always been her first priority and she felt no guilt in being exactly who she was.

A mother.

Always a mother.

As she came down the steps, Dean was there. He caught her in his arms and swung her around. She gazed into his loving eyes and suddenly realized the diploma wasn't her dream.

It was Dean.
It had always been Dean.
And she'd had the dream all along.

Love Inspired
HISTORICAL

*Powerful, engaging stories of romance,
adventure and faith set in the past—
when life was simpler and faith played a
major role in everyday lives.*

*See below for a sneak preview of
HIGH COUNTRY BRIDE
by Jillian Hart*

*Love Inspired Historical—
love and faith throughout the ages*

Silence remained between them, and she felt the rake of his gaze, taking her in from the top of her wind-blown hair where escaped tendrils snapped in the wind to the toe of her scuffed, patched shoes. She watched him fist up his big, work-roughened hands and expected the worst.

"You never told me, Miz Nelson. Where are you going to go?" His tone was flat, his jaw tensed as if he were still fighting his temper. His blue gaze shot past her to watch the children going about their picking up.

"I don't know." Her throat went dry. Her tongue felt thick as she answered. "When I find employment, I could wire a payment to you. Rent. Y-you aren't think-ing of bringing the sher-rif in?"

"You think I want *payment?*" He boomed like winter thunder. *"You think I want rent money?"*

"Frankly, I don't know what you want."

"I'll tell you what I don't want. I don't want—" His words cannoned in the silence as he paused, and a passing pair of geese overhead honked in flat-noted tones. He grimaced, and it was impossible to know what he would say or do.

She trembled, not from fear of him, she truly didn't believe he would strike her, but from the unknown. Of being forced to take the frightening step off the only safe spot she'd known since she'd lost Pa's house.

When you were homeless, everything seemed so fragile, so easily off balance, for it was a big, unkind world for a woman alone with her children. She had no one to protect her. No one to care. The truth was, she'd never had those things in her husband. How could she expect them from any stranger? Especially this man she hardly knew, who was harsh and cold and hardhearted.

And, worse, what if he brought in the law?

"You can't keep living out of a wagon," he said, still angry, the cords still straining in his neck. "Animals have enough sense to keep their young cared for and safe."

Yes, it was as she'd thought. He intended to be as cruel about this as he could be. She spun on her heel, pulling up all her defenses, and was determined to let his upcoming hurtful words roll off her like rainwater on an oiled tarp. She grabbed the towel the children had neatly folded and tossed it into the laundry box in the back of the wagon.

"Miz Nelson. I'm talking to you."

"Yes, I know. If you expect me to stand there while you tongue lash me, you're mistaken. I have packing to get to." Her fingers were clumsy as she hefted the bucket of water she'd brought for washing—she wouldn't need that now— and heaved.

His hand clasped on the handle beside hers, and she could feel the life and power of him vibrate along the thin metal. "Give it to me."

Her fingers let go. She felt stunned as he walked away, easily carrying the bucket that had been so heavy to her, and quietly, methodically, put out the small cooking fire. He did not seem as ominous or as intimidating—somehow—as he stood in the shadows, bent to his task, although she couldn't say why that was. Perhaps it was because he wasn't acting the way she was used to men acting. She was quite used to doing all the work.

Jamie scurried over, juggling his wooden horses, to watch. Daisy hung back, eyes wide and still, taking in the mysterious goings-on.

He is different when he's near to them, she realized. He didn't seem harsh, and there was no hint of anger—or, come to think of it, any other emotion—as he shook out the empty bucket, nodded once to the children and then retraced his path to her.

"Let me guess." He dropped the bucket onto the tailgate, and his anger appeared to be back. Cords strained in his neck and jaw as he growled at her. "If you leave here, you don't know where you're going and you have no money to get there with?"

She nodded. "Yes, sir."

"Then get you and your kids into the wagon. I'll hitch up your horses for you." His eyes were cold and yet they were not unfeeling as he fastened his gaze on hers. "I have an empty shanty out back of my house that no one's living in. You can stay there for the night."

"What?" She stumbled back, and the solid wood of the tailgate bit into the small of her back. "But—"

"There will be no argument," he bit out, interrupting her. "None at all. I buried a wife and son years ago, what was most precious to me, and to see you and them neglected like this—with no one to care—" His jaw ground again and his eyes were no longer cold.

Joanna didn't think she'd ever seen anything sadder than Aiden McKaslin as the sun went down on him.

* * * * *

*Don't miss this deeply moving story,
HIGH COUNTRY BRIDE,
available July 2008
from the new Love Inspired Historical line.*

*Also look for SEASIDE CINDERELLA
by Anna Schmidt,
where a poor servant girl and a
wealthy merchant prince
might somehow make a life together.*

REQUEST YOUR FREE BOOKS!

2 FREE NOVELS PLUS 2 FREE GIFTS!

HARLEQUIN®

Super Romance®

Exciting, emotional, unexpected!

YES! Please send me 2 FREE Harlequin Superromance® novels and my 2 FREE gifts (gifts are worth about $10). After receiving them, if I don't wish to receive any more books, I can return the shipping statement marked "cancel." If I don't cancel, I will receive 6 brand-new novels every month and be billed just $4.69 per book in the U.S. or $5.24 per book in Canada, plus 25¢ shipping and handling per book and applicable taxes, if any*. That's a savings of close to 15% off the cover price! I understand that accepting the 2 free books and gifts places me under no obligation to buy anything. I can always return a shipment and cancel at any time. Even if I never buy another book from Harlequin, the two free books and gifts are mine to keep forever.

135 HDN EEX7   336 HDN EEYK

Name	(PLEASE PRINT)	
Address		Apt. #
City	State/Prov.	Zip/Postal Code

Signature (if under 18, a parent or guardian must sign)

Mail to the Harlequin Reader Service:
IN U.S.A.: P.O. Box 1867, Buffalo, NY 14240-1867
IN CANADA: P.O. Box 609, Fort Erie, Ontario L2A 5X3

Not valid to current subscribers of Harlequin Superromance books.

Want to try two free books from another line?
Call 1-800-873-8635 or visit www.morefreebooks.com.

* Terms and prices subject to change without notice. N.Y. residents add applicable sales tax. Canadian residents will be charged applicable provincial taxes and GST. Offer not valid in Quebec. This offer is limited to one order per household. All orders subject to approval. Credit or debit balances in a customer's account(s) may be offset by any other outstanding balance owed by or to the customer. Please allow 4 to 6 weeks for delivery. Offer available while quantities last.

Your Privacy: Harlequin is committed to protecting your privacy. Our Privacy Policy is available online at www.eHarlequin.com or upon request from the Reader Service. From time to time we make our lists of customers available to reputable third parties who may have a product or service of interest to you. If you would prefer we not share your name and address, please check here. ☐

HSR08R

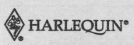

#1 NEW YORK TIMES
BESTSELLING AUTHOR
DEBBIE MACOMBER

What do you want most in the world?

Anne Marie Roche wants to find happiness again. At 38,
she's childless, a recent widow and alone. On Valentine's
Day, Anne Marie and several other widows get together to
celebrate…what? Hope, possibility, the future. They each
begin a list of twenty wishes.

Anne Marie's list includes learning to knit, doing good for
someone else and falling in love again. She begins to act on
her wishes, and when she volunteers at a school, little Ellen
enters her life. It's a relationship that becomes far more
important than she ever imagined, one in which they both
learn that wishes can come true.

Twenty Wishes

"These involving stories…continue the Blossom Street
themes of friendship and personal growth that readers
find so moving."—*Booklist* on *Back on Blossom Street*

Available the first week of May 2008 wherever books are sold!

MIRA®

Lawyer Audrey Lincoln has sworn off
love, throwing herself into her work
instead. When she meets a much younger
cop named Ryan Mercedes, all her logic
is tossed out the window, and Ryan is
determined that he will not let the issue
of age come between them. It is not until
a tragic case involving an innocent child
threatens to tear them apart that Ryan
and Audrey must fight for a way to
finally be together....

Look for

TRUSTING RYAN
by Tara Taylor Quinn

*Available July
wherever you buy books.*

SAVE $1.⁰⁰

A riveting trilogy from
BRENDA NOVAK

SAVE $1.⁰⁰ on the purchase price of one book in The Last Stand trilogy from Brenda Novak.

Offer valid from May 27, 2008, to August 30, 2008.
Redeemable at participating retail outlets. Limit one coupon per purchase.

Canadian Retailers: Harlequin Enterprises Limited will pay the face value of this coupon plus 10.25¢ if submitted by customer for this product only. Any other use constitutes fraud. Coupon is nonassignable. Void if taxed, prohibited or restricted by law. Consumer must pay any government taxes. Void if copied. Nielsen Clearing House ("NCH") customers submit coupons and proof of sales to Harlequin Enterprises Limited, P.O. Box 3000, Saint John, NB E2L 4L3, Canada. Non-NCH retailer—for reimbursement submit coupons and proof of sales directly to Harlequin Enterprises Limited, Retail Marketing Department, 225 Duncan Mill Rd., Don Mills, Ontario M3B 3K9, Canada.

U.S. Retailers: Harlequin Enterprises Limited will pay the face value of this coupon plus 8¢ if submitted by customer for this product only. Any other use constitutes fraud. Coupon is nonassignable. Void if taxed, prohibited or restricted by law. Consumer must pay any government taxes. Void if copied. For reimbursement submit coupons and proof of sales directly to Harlequin Enterprises Limited, P.O. Box 880478, El Paso, TX 88588-0478, U.S.A. Cash value 1/100 cents.

® and TM are trademarks owned and used by the trademark owner and/or its licensee.
© 2008 Harlequin Enterprises Limited

MBNTRI08CPN

HARLEQUIN Super Romance

COMING NEXT MONTH

#1500 TRUSTING RYAN • Tara Taylor Quinn
For Detective Ryan Mercedes, right and wrong are clear. And what he feels for guardian ad litem Audrey Lincoln is very right. Their shared pursuit of justice proves they're on the same side. But when a case divides them, can he see things her way?

#1501 A MARRIAGE BETWEEN FRIENDS • Melinda Curtis
Marriage of Inconvenience
They were friends who married when Jill needed a father for her unborn child, and Vince offered his name. Then, unexpectedly, Jill walked out. Now, eleven years later, Vince Patrizio is back to reclaim his wife...and the son who should have been theirs.

#1502 HIS SON'S TEACHER • Kay Stockham
The Tulanes of Tennessee
Nick Tulane has never fallen for a teacher. A former dropout, he doesn't go for the academic type. Until he meets Jennifer Rose, that is. While she's busy helping his son catch up at school, Nick starts wishing for some private study time with the tutor.

#1503 THE CHILD COMES FIRST • Elizabeth Ashtree
Star defense attorney Simon Montgomery is called upon to defend a girl who claims to be wrongly accused of murder. Her social worker Jayda Kavanagh believes she's innocent. But as Simon and Jayda grow close trying to save the child, Jayda's own youthful trauma could stand between her and the love Simon offers.

#1504 NOBODY'S HERO • Carrie Alexander
Count on a Cop
Massachusetts state police officer Sean Rafferty has sworn off ever playing hero again. All he wants is to be left alone to recover. Which is perfect, because Connie Bradford doesn't need a hero in her life. Unfortunately, her grieving daughter does...

#1505 THE WAY HOME • Jean Brashear
Everlasting Love
They'd been everything to each other. But Bella Parker—stricken with amnesia far from home—can't remember any of it...not even the betrayal that made her leave. Now James Parker has to decide how much of their past he should tell her. Because the one piece that could jog her memory might destroy them forever.